MAD AS A HATTER

IRIS LEIGH

Cover Design: Sleepy Fox Studio

Chapter Illustration: @ivonnii_art

Mad as a Hatter

Seeking a little excitement in life can sometimes lead to trouble.

At 37-years-old, life is good but not great. It's missing a little spark, so it's high time I do something to rectify that.

A move across the country to the town my grandparents called home is exactly what I've been missing. I'll embrace my magic, reopen their shop, and hope I don't get run out of a town. The good people of Snowton Heights believe the Wayward curse has returned with a vengeance. That might be true, but before I can find out for sure, I have another problem that needs my attention. A dead body on my front doorstep could derail my quest for a new life.

Contents

Chapter 1

"**S**erafina sweetie, there is nothing to be embarrassed about."

I nodded, rolling my eyes as I stood in the airport waiting for when we could board so I could hightail it out of New York City. It was time. I had nothing going for me here. At least not anymore.

"Your sisters will be so happy to have you closer!" my mother exclaimed as I tried to stuff my items back into my carry-on bag. The flight attendants just called for first class and I wished that could be me. But I was broke. Beyond broke. My mother was paying for my flight so I could leave the city that had been my home for over a decade.

"Mom, you can't tell Serena and Sabine. We talked about this."

A dejected sigh escaped my lips. We had talked about it. I knew she would keep my secret, but I also knew she really, like really, wanted to tell my family that I was back in the area. I just wasn't sure I was ready to face them.

"Sweetie, they won't care! They will be ecstatic!"

"I know ... I just..."

I just didn't know if I was ready to face them. I left a long time ago, and I felt bad for not being more part of their lives, but I had my own life to live. A perfect, normal, one that I couldn't do when being a Wayward. My family was the exact opposite of what could be considered normal. Like my mother.

"When you are ready, let me know. I'll plan a party! Oh, sweetie, I'm so excited you are going to embrace magic."

I bit my bottom lip as my mother continued talking. Was I fully embracing magic? *I don't think so.* Was I going to at least try? *Yeah.* I held up my keys as I looked at the new addition. It was the whole point I was flying to Seattle. Not to the heart of the city, but to a small suburb that not many people knew existed. Where my grandparents used to live and own a shop. I was going to re-open the shop.

Also, because I lost my job, got kicked out of my apartment by my roommate, and my boyfriend broke up with me. There was that.

I stretched out in my seat, making sure to work out the kinks in my legs. It would be the last time I had proper leg room for the next few hours. Cons of buying a cheap last-minute ticket out of here. Nothing I could do about it.

"Call me if you need anything, okay? Even if you just need to talk."

"Yes, Mom," I replied. It felt like I was a teenager again, instead of a woman in my late thirties. My mother nagging to make sure I knew she was there, that she loved me, then she would kiss my forehead and send me off to bed. Even though I disliked it slightly, it was what I needed, some sense of normalcy since my life had been turned upside down—though my mother was the furthest thing from normal.

I grabbed my bag, hauling it over my shoulders as I went to go stand in line. The flight attendants had finally called for my zone to board. I couldn't help but play with the ticket in my hand. This was my ticket out of here. And to think, just yesterday I had fled from Seattle away from the craziness. Away from the magic. To the hustle and bustle of New York City. My dreams carrying me all the way till

I landed on my feet and for a time I had achieved what people would have considered normal. I couldn't afford to live on my own. I had a roommate—this was New York City, after all—but I had a loving boyfriend, an amazing job, and a normal life. Or so I thought.

"Ticket, please." A lady with hair pulled back into a low bun, a handkerchief wrapped around her neck, reached for my ticket. A piece of paper I gladly handed over. Quickly placing it facedown on the scanner, it popped green for a moment and she ushered me forward, handing the ticket back to me. As I followed behind the other to board the plane, the knot in my chest loosened. The sadness at losing my life here didn't leave instantly as I boarded the plane, but it got better. In time, I would pick up the pieces of my life and start anew.

Glancing down at my ticket, I located my seat number before looking around the plane to figure out my seat. A middle seat. I guess it was a little too much to ask to have the magic kick in now and grant me an aisle seat. That was asking for too much, as I had left magic behind and never looked back. Till my life had been a dumpster fire and I needed a miracle. A magical one. That was when I realized I had tried to outrun it, tried to suppress it and forget it, but the thing about magic is that it exists. Regardless if you believe in it or not, it's out there, just waiting for the perfect moment. The moment to beckon me home. And I had answered.

"Sorry, I'm in the middle seat."

A businessman sitting in the aisle seat with his laptop already out, rapidly typing away, looked up briefly. He let loose a long huff as he slammed his laptop closed, unbuckled his belt, and stood up slightly, only to lean back in his seat to let me get by.

It was awkward. Having to put his tray up and hold it since I didn't click it into place. The glares the man was sending me had me fumbling to complete the simplest of tasks as I squeezed by him—only stepping on his toes once. Okay, maybe twice in the process of getting to my seat. With backpack in hand, I slid it under the seat before relaxing. This was really my life now. I was really going to be starting over.

"Hi, I'm Kat, but with a k."

"Serafina," I replied as I shook the lady's hand who had already claimed the window seat. She looked to be in her twenties, but I wasn't sure about her exact age other than she was younger than me.

"You seem like a cat person."

"Excuse me?" I replied.

"Sorry. I spend way more time with cats than people, more than I care to admit sometimes."

"Oh, no problem," I muttered as I wiggled in my seat, trying to get comfortable for the long flight ahead.

"I'm going to Seattle for fun. I need a vacation."

She seemed friendly enough, so I replied, "I'm starting over."

"Any practical reason? Divorce? Job? Change of scenery."

"I guess all three of them in a weird way," I answered. While I hadn't been married, we were practically married. Been together for six years and all of it ended in a single night. No gentle tearing off the Band-Aid, it was just ripped off in one go since he couldn't see a future with someone who couldn't hold down a job.

"You should get a cat. There is just something magical about them. They come to you even when you don't want them." Kat turned towards me, her eyes rolling slightly. "Trust me, I know."

I furrowed my eyebrows together, pursing my lips. Kat was an odd one. Though her name fit.

"Don't mind me, I have gotten used to talking to cats." Kat paused, her eyes wide. "Not talking, just talking about them. Anyway ... have a pleasant flight." She turned towards the window and peered outside, leaving me to myself as the flight attendant went over the flight safety demonstration. This was it. I was officially on my way to Seattle.

Chapter 2

"You have family out here?"

I cast a glance over to the bus driver, who was looking at me through the rearview mirror. He held my gaze for a moment before going back to focusing on the road. The vehicle jerked as we increased in speed in an attempt to climb the hill. Seattle's hilly roads were one thing I didn't miss.

"Kind of," I replied to the man, his green eyes glancing at me in the mirror briefly.

"Kind of? Like they dead or you don't talk to them?"

I bit my lip. "Both," I answered. It was true. I had family scattered throughout Washington. My sisters were in the city, but in the heart of it, instead of in a no-name subdivision far from all the attractions that tourists thought of when thinking of the Emerald City.

"Ah, first time here or been here before?"

I smiled at the bus driver, whose eyebrows shot up in surprise. It was just the two of us on the bus. The last I remembered, few people visited Snowton Heights, and it still seemed to ring true. But I was happy he was providing comfort. This was a tremendous leap I was doing, moving across the country to reopen my grandparents' shop.

"Been here before. My grandparents used to live here."

"Oh, really?" His voice took on a higher pitch, signaling his surprise. "My wife is from here but we moved closer to the university due to all the bus routes. Cheaper housing over there than trying to live on Capitol Hill."

I nodded. It was expensive to live near the attractions that drew in tourists.

"Moving in or just visiting for..." His eyes glanced down to my suitcase and bag. "...a while?"

I couldn't help but glance down at my items as well. It wasn't common to travel with as much luggage as I did, but I had a whole life to pack up after all. It wasn't like I was going to be able to go back to my life in New York anymore. There was nothing waiting for me on that side of the country, only misery.

"Moving. I'm re-opening my grandparents' shop."

The bus screeched to a halt as we reached a red light. The bus driver turned in his chair so his body was pointed towards me.

"Oh yeah? What was the name of their shop? I'll ask my wife about it. Maybe we will even stop by when we are in town."

"Wayward Shop of Mysteries," I replied, the name just rolling off my tongue like it was the most natural thing in the world. And I guess it was. Wayward was my last name. It was the *shop of mysteries* that should have felt foreign. But it wasn't. Magic coursed through my bloodline, but Grandma thought it would be too obvious to use the world magic in the name. No reason to paint a target on our back that we were witches. Back then, it wasn't as easy to proclaim being a witch as it is today. Though it's still hard.

"Oh really? Never heard of it. I will definitely have to bring the wife over one day."

The man turned back to the road as the light had finally turned green, the bus jerking forward once more, causing my body to slide slightly forward. I held out my hand, pressing it against the seat in front of me, preventing myself from sliding any more.

"Please do. Not sure when I'll be officially open for business."

That was the big if. It all depended on the shop and how badly it had been neglected. The only thing I knew was that it wasn't a broken-down shack, or my mom wouldn't have proposed this. She knew I wasn't handy, and with magic it might have been easier to fix it up, but I didn't have magic. Not after ignoring it for so long. That was the next hurdle. Even if the shop was in good condition, I had to somehow get in tune with my magic to create items to sell. All of it was easier said than done.

"Well, lady, we are almost at our last stop. Snowton Heights," he called back as he turned a corner, a bus sign up ahead popping up in the headlights. I looked out the window, taking in the city. Last time I had been here was as a child. And didn't look like much had changed in the years I had been gone. It still felt like a town in the middle of nowhere.

The bus screeched to a halt, the brakes groaning. I stood, grabbing my bags as the doors opened. The bus driver once more turned in his seat, only this time he got up and helped me maneuver my bags off the bus and onto the sidewalk.

"Have a good night and be safe out there."

"Will do, thank you Mr....?"

"Just call me Garrett."

"Well, thank you, Garrett. Have a wonderful night. I can't wait for you to stop by the shop. That is once I figure out how to open it."

Garrett waved goodbye as he made his way back onto the bus, calling out over his shoulder one last time before closing the doors and leaving me alone on the sidewalk.

"Oh, don't worry! I'm sure you will be great!"

I could only hope so.

Chapter 3

I watched the bus take off down the road until it turned the corner and disappeared out of sight before grabbing my bags. Or attempting to. I lunged forward, trying to catch my suitcase as it fell into the street. One wheel had gotten caught in the crack of the road.

"Get out of the street, old lady!"

A man stuck his head out the window, his arm following after him as he held up his middle finger before zooming past and disappearing down the same road the bus had. I didn't waste another moment and grabbed the handle of my suitcase to drag it out of danger and back to the sidewalk. I guess Snowton Heights wasn't a ghost town after all if they had such lively people prowling around at night. It also wasn't the most welcoming either, not at all how I remembered.

With a deep sigh, I tugged my suitcase while clutching my bag over my shoulder and made my way down the street, my feet going on autopilot towards the shop. It was late, and I should head to where I would be sleeping, but a part of me wanted to see the shop. I had a tingling feeling in my chest.

The farther I walked from the bus shop, the quieter it got. Thankfully, I had been dropped off on the strip, the only good thing in Snowton Heights. It was where everything and anything was located, including the Wayward Shop of Mysteries. As if sensing how close I was coming to the place my grandparents loved more than life itself, my pace quickened, fueled by curiosity and a small part by hope—hope that I hadn't turned my life into even more of a dumpster fire by taking on something impossible. It was already bad enough that...

The self-doubt thoughts halted as I stared at the familiar sign of my childhood. My pace slowed as I took in the shop I hadn't seen in years. A part of me felt like it was just yesterday, helping my grandparents, and yet a part of me felt like it was thousands of years ago.

Despite only half the sign being readable, there was no doubt this was the Wayward Shop of Mysteries. The new chapter of my life was about to start. I dragged my suitcase the final distance to stand in front of the window as I marveled at the place I had spent a decent amount of my childhood.

The top of the sign, which read *Wayward*, usually lit up by bulbs, would shine in the moonlight, but not tonight. That was already one item on my list to fix before we opened. Though the second part was just painted in white shone because of the moonlight and streetlights.

"That shop hasn't been open in years."

A scream ripped from my throat as I turned on my heels to face the person who'd snuck up on me. He stood two heads taller than me, his hands on his hips, lips curved up in a grin. I placed a hand on my chest, trying to still my beating heart. He didn't look dangerous, but still ... approaching a female at night ... *alone*?

"I know," I muttered as I patted my pocket, feeling my set of keys. *Just in case*, I told myself. One could never be too careful.

"If you are looking to buy any souvenirs, you are best looking elsewhere, unless you want to wait a decade or two."

His laugh was boisterous, disarming, as I took in his green eyes. He reached behind his neck, rubbing at it as he noticed me staring at him. For some reason, I could feel my lips curving upward in a smile. Having a conversation with a stranger at night in the middle of nowhere wasn't exactly how I imagined starting this new chapter of my life. But it was the perfect time to try new things.

The man shifted, walking past me as he gazed into the shop.

The place that was now mine.

"Every time I look in there, it just gets dustier," he muttered as he almost pressed his face to the glass and glanced around. Even though I had no idea who he was, I could feel the heat rising to my cheeks. I touched them, and they were hot, surprising since the wind blasting against my face was cold, reminding me that I was still in the north—and yet here was a stranger lighting me on fire from embarrassment from how unkept the place was. The man let loose a whistle as he leaned back, shoving his hands into his pockets. His green eyes landed back on me.

"It's too bad. I heard this place used to be very popular."

"Really?" The word was out before I could even think about it. I wanted to hear about the shop after being away for so long.

"I wasn't here when it was open but I heard some good things," he answered as he took another glance into the shop. "Along with some bad stuff."

"Bad stuff?" I quietly muttered under my breath. What was he talking about? I had never heard anything negative about my grandparents. I thought they were loved by the people for their mystical items.

He pointed to my suitcase. "New in town or here for a trip?"

I glanced down at my suitcase. Did people actually come to Snowton Heights to visit?

"Moving here. But bad stuff? What do you mean?" I inquired. All I could do was hope it wasn't something so outlandish that I would be forced to leave town before actually having a chance to start anew. It would be worse to actually start and have it ripped from me.

Just like New York.

"Best not to be spreading the bad rumors around. Though there is a particular rumor about a new owner in town, but that has been going around for ages." He motioned to the shop. "And yet it remains closed."

"There is a rumor that there is a new owner?"

"Yeah. It's a mystery to who, actually. If you think about it, mysterious owner for a shop of mysteries." The guy let loose another round of laughter, bringing another smile to my face. So far, I was two for three on meeting nice people since my arrival in Snowton Heights. Already I could feel this was going to be different. I wouldn't be making the same mistakes I did when I first ran off to New York.

"Well, it can't be that mysterious if people already know about the new owner. How did that rumor start?"

"Hard to hide messing with the utilities for a place that hasn't needed it in years."

I nodded. It was the utilities that had ratted me out. Mom must have sent people over to make sure everything was on and functional for my arrival, so it would be one less thing to worry about. I had to make sure to call her later to thank her once again. She was the true star, standing strong even when I wanted to crumble.

"Are people excited about it opening up?" I asked. I looked in the shop, noticing all the dust he had mentioned earlier.

"Some are," he started, joining me as we both stared in the glass window. "There are some who aren't. Me? I'm just excited to have a new neighbor."

I paused, turning to look at the man, who was still peering into the Wayward shop of Mysteries. *Neighbor?* I glanced around, looking at the shops that lined the block on both sides. Did he also have a business?

The only way I would be able to find out was if I asked: "Neighbor?"

"Yeah, I'm across the street," he answered, jerking a thumb over his shoulder to the shop that stood directly across from us. The shop was a cute pastel tone, with the building being a light blue, while the sign above it was written in an assortment of colors. Sweet Tokens of Sugar. Just by the name, it had to be a bakery or candy shop. Something that served sugary delights. The lights in the shop were dimmed, but I could make out a line of glass display cases. There was definitely something sweet over there.

"You work there?" I inquired. It was never good to judge a book by its cover, but the man standing beside me just didn't scream pastry chef or candy maker. Standing two heads taller than me, his green eyes bored into me as he peered down. His lips curved slightly upward as if he knew where my train of thought was going. His smile brought my gaze up to his eyebrows, where there was a line going through his left one. Was it a scar or design? Something I felt would be too rude to ask. Then there was the dark curly hair bouncing softly with the light breeze. But it was only curly on top, as the sides were kept short by having a fade.

"I own it."

Oh.

That was why he had looked amused when I had been taking him in. Heat raised back to my cheeks at jumping to the quick assumption. It was my second time judging him tonight, too.

"My name is Warren." He reached out his hand to me, interrupting all other thoughts about how I had jumped the gun. His name felt like it suited him. "What's your name?"

"Serafina," I blurted, thankful that he had changed the topic. So we wouldn't have to talk about how I had judged him. With his hand still held out, I shook it. His grip was firm, his hand almost swallowing my own.

"So, Serafina..." His lips curved upward into a smile once more, his green eyes shining under the moonlight. "...why move here?"

There it was. A question I didn't even know I was dreading to answer. It was one thing to internally vocalize that I would be opening the Wayward Shop of Mysteries. That after years of being closed, I was the new owner. But it was an entirely different thing to vocalize it verbally in the real world.

"Well..." I started, "it's because of this shop," I muttered as I waved to the glass window that we had been peering into.

"This shop? Hopefully, you don't have anything to return or you might just be out of luck." Warren once more let loose a boisterous laugh, scratching at the back of his neck. His laugh was so disarming and it was right then and there I decided to put effort into making Warren my friend. It also helped that he owned the business across the street and it wouldn't take going through different boroughs to hang out. It was a simple road I could cross with just a few steps and a glance both ways.

"Not an item to return per se, but I am returning," I answered in a roundabout way, still prolonging the declaration of exactly why I was in Snowton Heights. Warren shifted his gaze as he took in the shop before looking at me and then back at the shop.

"By chance..." he started, but I already knew where his train of thought was going and I smiled. It seems we were both able to catch each other off guard.

"Yeah, I'm the new owner."

"Well then..." He let out a nervous laugh, unlike his loud ones before. "...that would explain why you were peering into the window at night." He took a step back from the shop, inching his way towards the road. "You have some big shoes to fill. I heard a lot of wonderful things about this place. I can't wait to see what you do with it."

"Thanks," I muttered back shyly, caught off guard by the praise. We didn't know each other and yet here was basically telling me I was going to be great. "It might be hard at first, but hopefully it will get easier." That was all I could hope for. I had left everything behind in New York to start anew, and already it was looking better. Surely, if I had already hit rock bottom, it would only be up from here.

"If you need anything, you know where to find me." He jerked a thumb over his shoulder to his shop. "Now, I do need to get back to closing up. Now that I've confirmed you aren't a thief."

My mouth dropped open as he waved goodbye and scurried across the street, his larger-than-life laughter erupting as he took a glance over his shoulder, giving me another wave before dipping into his shop.

With my need to see the shop filled, there was no other reason to stay standing on the side of the road. Taking a hold of my luggage, I headed towards where I would be staying, fully intent on passing out as soon as my body landed against something soft. First day back in Snowton Heights had been a success.

Chapter 4

"You got to be kidding me," I hollered, only for a string of coughs to erupt. After my fit, my chest hurt and my throat burned as I tried to cover my nose and mouth, my eyes still bearing the blunt force of all the dust that had accumulated in the shop since I had been gone. I had been foolish. Without thinking, I had popped the key into the door, unlocked it and thrown it open, hoping to be greeted by my new future, but all there was was dust, more dust, and even more dust if that was even possible. And it was. Somehow.

"Sweet dusty nostalgia."

I gazed about the shop, images of what it looked like in its prime flashing before my eyes. So vastly different, and yet it had the same warmth. Not the feeling of coming home after being gone forever, but more like seeing a long-lost friend after years apart. That kind of swirling feeling inside where we could have not talked for months, even years, but the second we were back together, it was like no time had passed at all.

"Where to even start?" I muttered to myself, mouth and nose still covered, as I stepped deeper into the store. The bookshelves still stood in the same spot from when I had been here last, creating a row towards the counter that stood in the middle of the shop, where even more shelves lay scatted behind it. It wasn't huge, and it wasn't overly small, just a decent sized shop. Perfect for new owners. Absolutely perfect for me.

I ran my finger across one of the bookshelves. "Very dusty … so dusty," I cried as I wiped the grime on my pants. Somehow I would need to find a way to roll back time to clean up this place and restore it to its previous glory. If only I had magic.

Butterflies swirled inside as I made my way deeper into the shop, the dust swarming around me with every step I took. It was rustic in here, a lot of the pieces wooden instead of metal. An ode to nature, my grandmother liked to say. But that wasn't why there were butterflies swarming inside. It was because of the door in the back. Regular people thought it was a storage area where all the extra product was kept. But I knew better.

"Hello, old friend."

I ran my fingers across the wooden door; it had been shut for years.

Gently, I reached for the doorknob, part of me scared of the state the room would be in, but another part glad that I was getting to see my friend again. A jolt coursed through my hand, passing through my body. I hadn't remembered this part from my childhood, but I wasn't sure if I had ever actually opened the door by myself before, always just trailing behind someone.

When the jolt disappeared and there was no longer a buzz in my body, I tugged it open. The door protesting, letting out a loud creak at finally being cracked open after being neglected for so long, dust slammed into my face as I took a step in. I coughed again; my throat burned. Dust might actually be the death of me before I could even start on this new chapter of my life.

"Everything looks the same as I remembered … only smaller," I muttered as I took in the back room. Memories flashed before me of how I used to run through the shop, giggling as I did so, chasing after my grandmother in an attempt to watch her work her magic. How we would gather around the cauldron in the middle of the room and she would drop ingredients into it as the liquid bubbled and spilled over the top.

A smile formed on my face as I thought about that one time. I had got a tongue thrashing from my grandfather for almost falling into the pot when my grandmother had turned her back. He had told me if I fell in, I would be turned into a frog and I would have to wait till my prince charming came and rescued me before I would be human again. Something I didn't like as a kid for multiple reasons. Frogs weren't even on my list of favorite beings and still aren't. And the thought of waiting around for someone else to rescue me wasn't ideal.

"Now, where are your grimoires?" I asked out loud. I glanced around, taking the shop with the cauldron in the middle. Boxes were scattered about on the floor, on the shelves, and on the table. Eventually, I would have to sift through all of it to clean out the place. But most importantly to find my grandmother's grimoires. Without those, I would have a hard time learning magic. It would be utterly impossible. Magic didn't call to me like it did to my other family members. It just wasn't as natural as others would have hoped. Something I had used as an excuse to stop practicing in my attempt to have a normal life.

"Maybe in here?" I questioned as I lifted the lid off the first box in sight—regretting my decision almost instantly as a layer of grime covered my hand and dust filled the air, making me sneeze. *So much dust ... so much...* The shop would have to be cleaned from head to toe before I felt comfortable opening up. Because if I opened up as it, it would be a health risk not just for myself but the customers too. When the layer of dust in the air had settled, I peered into the box to be greeted by a giant crystal ball.

"Well, that's not what I was looking for."

I picked up the giant crystal ball and peered at the glass. The surface rippled for a moment before stilling. I couldn't help but frown. At least it showed I had magic, as the crystal ball responded to my touch, but the fact it had gone still so quickly showed just how much skill I was lacking.

If only I hadn't shunned it...

I shook the thoughts from my head. It would do no good to be thinking about all the what-ifs. The past couldn't be rewritten. All I could do was move forward. It was a new chapter of my life. And that meant being kinder to myself. Not forcing myself to fit in, and especially not bringing myself down due to something out of my control.

My body froze as I felt something crawling across my hand and down my arm. I zeroed in on the little bug, a little grayish thing with extremely large legs. Not caring that I was a thousand times bigger than it, it zoomed down my forearm towards my biceps. Before it could latch on to my clothes and disappear to cause even more havoc, I gained my senses and screamed. Shifting the crystal ball to one hand as I used my other to smack at my arm in hopes of killing the little creature. Only doing enough to scare it and causing it to fall to the floor as it scurried off.

"I hate spiders!" I hollered as I hopped from foot to foot, unsure of where exactly it had disappeared. After a few minutes, and after calming my rapidly beating heart, I calmed down and set the crystal ball back in the box.

"I will have to look through all of this another day."

Because there was no way I was subjecting myself to more spiders.

Chapter 5

"Hello? Anyone in here?"

I turned towards the door that led to the front of the shop. The high-pitched and squeaky voice sounded like a little girl. Surely this place wasn't haunted, right? I pursed my lips as I walked away from the cauldron and the million boxes to go back to the front to confront whoever else was crazy enough to walk into this death trap where dust and spiders were waiting to assault their next victim. A shiver coursed through my body. I was really not a fan of spiders.

"Hellooooooooooo?"

Now it sounded like a ghost as I quickly made my way out of the back room, making sure to close the door behind me, jiggling the doorknob for a second to confirm the door had locked itself. Good thing this door seemed to have its own magic and didn't rely on my own. I wouldn't have been able to lock the door, giving whoever the voice belonged to a chance to sneak into the back if they really wanted to. It was better for normal people to think this place was just mysterious and not magical.

"Helloooooooo?"

This time the voice sounded annoyed as I exclaimed, "One moment!" Satisfied that the door was locked, I turned towards the front to meet my guest. A head popped out from behind a bookcase, confirming that it was a little girl that had been calling out to me. Without missing a beat, she stepped out from behind the bookcase and made her way over to stand right in front of me. Her lips curled into a big smile, exposing a missing tooth, as she tilted her head back in order to stare at me.

"Hi, I'm April and I'm nine," she exclaimed as she shoved her hand out, her light brown hair swinging from side to side as she could not stand still.

"Hi there." I grasped her hand and shook it slowly as she nodded her head. "I'm Serafina." While it was nice to meet April, she shouldn't be out and about by herself. Her parents had to be worried sick about where she had run off to. It would be no good for them to discover her in a shop filled with years of neglect.

"Dad and I brought you some baked goods to welcome you to the neighborhood!"

I let go of April's hand in order to put my hands on my hips. Her dad? Baked goods? I had only arrived in Snowton Heights yesterday and encountered two people that I would classify as friendly. Garret and Warren. Warren had a bakery and lived in the neighborhood, which aligned with more of what April had said. I crouched in order to be closer to April's height as I placed my hands on my knees to see if I had guessed her parent correctly.

"By chance..." I started, hoping that if I guessed incorrectly that she didn't just blurt out a random name, because then I would surely be in a pickle. "Is your father Warren?"

The bell above the door jingled and I looked up to see someone pushing it open, their head down as they fumbled with a box in their hands.

"April, you aren't supposed to run off by yourself!" Warren shouted. He made a beeline straight towards the little girl, who crossed her arms over her chest and looked up at her father with an annoyed look.

"You were taking too long!"

"Doesn't matter, don't run off like that," Warren replied softly as he patted April's head, taking any all of her annoyance in an instant as she reached for the box.

"Here you go! It's for you!" April exclaimed as she twirled on her feet to face me and shoved the little blue box into my hands. "Open it up!"

I looked at the blue box that had a red ribbon wrapped around it as I smiled at the little girl who had yet to lose her own big smile. "Thank you, April, this looks fancy."

"Thanks, I added the ribbon."

"Technically, I added the ribbon because you ran off," Warren butted in, drawing a pout from April.

"It was my idea," she muttered.

"Regardless, it is wonderful. Thank you," I said, preventing any bickering. I wrapped my hand around the red ribbon in order to untie it, I didn't just want to rip it off. Not after their hard work to make it presentable.

"Hurry, hurry!" April whined as she bounced up and down beside me. As I quickened my pace to untie the ribbon and lift the lid of the box, a sweet aroma filled the air and assaulted my nose, and I couldn't help but lick my lips. It smelled wonderful. Like heaven on earth.

"Oh wow!" I squeaked, as they had certainly outdone themselves when presenting a welcome-to-the-neighborhood gift. I was so lucky to have met nice people, but confirming that Warren indeed knew how to bake was the icing on the cake. Speaking of cake, I didn't spot a slice in the box, but I did zero in on a cookie that had cinnamon sprinkled on it. I removed the small cookie to take a bite.

"Sand tarts. Those are our best sellers."

I could see why. They were simple yet hypnotizing, drawing my attention instantly. They didn't look overly sweet but sweet enough that you could munch on whenever. Licking my lips once more, I bit into the cookie and my body shut down. Flavor erupted in my mouth, my body relaxing as I shoved the rest of the cookie in my face. It might not have looked ladylike to scarf down a cookie, but there was no reason for Warren to produce something so amazing.

"I want one!" April shouted, her hand reaching up to poke at the box, only to get smacked away by Warren.

"You have them all the time at the store."

I smiled. They were adorable together. And even though Warren was right that April had an endless supply of these thanks to the amazing creator of these treats being her father, I still handed her one of the sand tarts. It was impossible to say no to her pouting face. Picking up another sand tart, I did an imaginary cheers with April, before we both scarfed down the wonderful small treats.

Having Warren as a neighbor was a double-edged sword. On one hand, it was great, because whenever I craved something sweet I knew I would be in excellent hands by just going across the street. But that also meant whenever I wanted a sugary snack there were no barriers stopping me from indulging in them. It wasn't like I was overweight, but I was definitely not skinny. According to the last time I went to the doctor, I was in the healthy range of weight, but I was closer to the edge than he would like. And indulging in sweets 24/7 was a sure way to send me across the line.

"You like them?" Warren asked, as if he hadn't just watched me down two cookies in an instant.

"Of course," I replied.

"Whenever you want some more, just stop on by. We sell those in little bags as people like to give them as gifts."

I shouldn't have made a mental note of his comment. I didn't need more sand tarts in my life, but I knew I wouldn't be able to resist the sweet cinnamon delights.

"There's more." Warren shifted so his shoulder brushed against mine as he pointed to the next item that had been next to the nonexistent sand tarts. "Two flavors of cake bites, strawberry and lemon. We have other flavors in the shop, but April picked those out for you."

"Those are my favorite!"

The lemon cake bite had white frosting on it with yellow sprinkles on top. The strawberry one had pink frosting with a white drizzle on top. Both looked absolutely amazing, and there was no doubt in my mind I would be devouring both of them as soon as Warren left. Until then, I couldn't stuff my face with all the sweets, no matter how bad I wanted to.

"And this?" I asked as I pointed to the next item in the box.

"Jam-topped mini cheesecake. This actually has three flavors. Apricot..." Warren pointed to the orange section. "Raspberry..." He motioned to the purple side before settling on the blue. "And blueberry. Again, not sure what you like, so I made a mini special one that had several flavors on it."

Was it possible to fall in love with sweets? I wasn't sure, but I was starting to think so. Raspberry cheesecake: I'd had one before, but apricot and blueberry I hadn't. And now I had the chance to have all three. My mouth watered as my stomach twisted into knots. Warren had really thought out this welcome gift, and I had nothing in return. I glanced around the shop, trying to spot anything that would do, but all that greeted me was dust and the occasional flicker of a bug crawling. None of it sounded like a good gift.

"And finally, stuffed in the corner since it barely fit in the box, is a mini peanut butter sandwich cookie," Warren said as he pointed to the last item. "Again, we weren't sure what you liked so we just stuffed a few things in there for you to try." Warren nodded to himself as if he were pleased before pausing, his eyes growing wide, "You aren't allergic to nuts or anything right? Probably should have asked that first before handing you food." He let loose an awkward laugh as he scratched at the back of his neck.

"No, I'm not," I answered.

"Just had to make sure. A dead body first day in town is not a good look."

"That is very true," I responded as I closed the lid to the blue box, fully intent on diving into the sugary delights when I was alone, away from both human and bugs. "I really appreciate this. It's a wonderful welcoming gift."

"Alright, she has her food!" April shouted as she latched on to her father's arm and started to drag him towards the front of the shop. Now let's go!"

Warren let himself be dragged by his daughter towards the door, the bell jingling as she opened it. "It seems we have to go! I signed April up for some classes in hopes of finding her a hobby!" It was comical watching the grown man be dragged out of the shop, only for him to grab hold of the frame and popping his head back in the shop as April dug her heels into the ground in her attempt to keep pulling him away. "Enjoy the sweets! Maybe we can catch up later?" Warren's voice filled up the shop in order to make sure I heard everything he said. I nodded and waved goodbye as he did his own little wave, removing his hand from the doorframe, effectively letting the little girl continue on her mission of tugging him down the street and out of view.

Chapter 6

I reached back into the blue box, intent on having a bite of cake now that I didn't have human company. No one was around to judge me other than the bugs.

"You a Wayward?"

My hand froze, hovering over the strawberry cake, as I slowly turned towards the front door. I had been so focused on the sugary delights that I hadn't heard the jingle above the door go off when the man cracked the door open, poking his head into the shop. With regret, I removed my hand from the box to put the lid back on it. The universe was telling me not to eat it even though I really wanted to.

"I am," I replied to the man. Now that I had confirmed who I was, he had taken it as an invitation to enter the shop fully. Unlike Warren, he was a few inches shorter than me. He had medium-length blond hair that was parted straight down the middle and slicked back with gel. A little too much gel, as there was no movement at all to his hair as he stepped to stand in front of me. "Can I help you? We aren't exactly open yet," I said, letting loose a nervous laugh as I motioned to the shop, letting him know this dusty place wasn't anywhere close to being open for business.

"I guess the rumor is true."

"Rumor?" I asked, tilting my head to the side. What rumor could have possibly sprouted and spread already when I had only arrived late last night? He had to have the wrong person. I had barely had time to meet people enough to elicit a rumor.

"I don't know why you came here," he snarled. Instantly, I took a step back from the crazed man as a coldness passed through my body, a heavy feeling in the pit of my stomach. I furrowed my brow. Was he missing a few marbles?

"What? I came here to open up this shop."

"The last thing we need in town is another Wayward!"

His words came out like a growl as he pressed forward, closing the distance between us, his breath hot against my skin. I attempted to lean back in order to put some distance between us but my body bumped into the counter behind me. Just a moment ago, I was inhaling the sweet aroma of a sugary treat, and now I was being assaulted by the smell of a crazed person.

"Look, I don't..." I started in my attempt to calm him down before he jumped off the edge, but his nostrils flared, his breathing coming out in huffs, baring his teeth to me, had silenced all words from my mouth. This man was a wild animal.

"Your family..." he started, words changing into a hiss. "...your kind..." he huffed as his voice grew in volume, "...is not welcome here!"

So that is what this is about.

He had a problem with witches and magic. But us being witches was just superstition to regular people, because believing in magic was still rare. There was no way he knew for a fact about my family being actual witches.

Play it cool.

"I'm not sure what you are talking about," I said softly, not trying to poke the already angered bear before me as he descended closer to a rampage.

"Leave Snowton!" he hollered, shoving a finger in my face. "Get lost!"

Without thinking, I opened my mouth, "I can't exactly leave, I have nowhere else to go." It was true, but it wasn't like he needed to know. "Maybe we should talk this out?" Like talking to a rabid animal was a smart idea. But my refusal had caused him a slight pause, giving me enough to wiggle out from between him and the counter and get behind it in order to put something between us. Just in case things went south.

And it did.

His fists slammed on the counter, sending shockwaves through my body. His nostrils flared rapidly as his breathing grew heavy. He pointed a finger directly in my face. "Get lost or you will regret it!"

We stood staring at each other for a moment as I tried to control my breathing. There was something wrong with him and I felt just existing around him was not a good idea. He turned on his heels, his slicked-back blond hair not moving an inch as he stomped his way out of my dusty shop, the anger pooling off him in waves, palpable. It felt like the building shook with every step he took. He jerked the door open, paused in order to send a glare my way, before stepping outside and slamming the door behind him. The bell above the door jingled like crazy at being manhandled.

Am I dreaming?

I must be, because that was absolutely crazy. My mouth had grown dry in his presence. I rubbed at my temples.

Never in my life had I been on the receiving end of such hatred. Sure, I had seen other people receive treatment. My old boss sure knew how to anger people. But it was never me. And yet one full day in town and I had already angered someone.

I placed my hand on my heart. I felt it thumping wildly against my chest. I glanced outside to confirm the man had truly left when I locked eyes with a lady just as bewildered as I. Had she heard everything that had unfolded just a moment ago? If that was the chance, a knot formed in my stomach, because that meant I hadn't been dreaming. With a shaky hand, I waved at the lady and mustered a smile. After which she took off like a bullet down the street and out of sight.

Well, okay, then.

This day had started off great with a sugary box of delights, only to take a full 180 with a rabid man breathing down my neck, and it wasn't even noon!

Chapter 7

It took from sun up to past sundown to clean up the place. Two days in total. A very long two days where my body protested all the movement of trying to clean every nook and cranny during the hunt to eradicate all bugs. Years of abandonment were scraped away with elbow grease, so much that I couldn't produce any more, then I sat down at the chair behind the counter. Relief seeped into my bones as I thought about my progress. The front was pretty much clean, but the back room was still dirty.

There was nothing fun about cleaning, but it had to be done. In order to move along on this new chapter of my life, I needed this place to be spotless in order to open for business. Which meant cleaning up the back room as soon as I got some rest. Or at least that is what I told myself as I closed my eyes. Instantly, my mind drifted towards those sand tarts Warren had given me. I had successfully managed to acquire no new sweets for the two days, but my supply was already running low from what was still remaining from my welcome-to-the-neighborhood gift.

"Serafina Wayward?"

The bell above the door jingled and I groaned. *Why now?* Why did someone decide to stop by now when I was just about to devour the cinnamon cookie?

"Serafina Wayward?" the person repeated and I let loose a sigh, shifting my head away from the nook of my elbow so I could crack open an eye to see who had stopped by. Only as soon as I took in the man's form, I jerked up, my chair stumbling over from the sudden movement, and I waited to see why I was being graced with a police officer's presence.

Pulling my shoulders back, I tried to straighten out my posture. I smoothed down my hair with one hand and used the other to rub the tiredness from my eyes.

"I see the shop is coming along," the police officer said as he inched his way closer to where I stood, his head on a swivel as he took in the shop.

"Yes, it is. I'm sorry it's still not open yet, though. Is there something I can help you with?"

The man continued to put one foot in the other, his hand reaching out to one of the bookcases to drag a finger against the wood. He stopped to inspect it before rubbing any residue that may have lingered away.

"Not bad..." He let loose an appreciative whistle. "Glad to see this place is being whipped back into code."

Was having dust in the store against the code? I wasn't sure, but good thing I spent so much time taking care of the place. He examined a few more bookcases, running his finger against them to truly confirm that the dirt had disappeared. When he was satisfied, he set his sights on me, reached for a notebook in his breast pocket. With a quick lick of his finger, he flipped open to a page and clicked his pen before shooting a grin in my direction.

Somehow I managed to plaster a smile on my face, but I knew I was only smiling because this was awkward and I wasn't sure why the police officer was here, but if he was taking notes, then it seemed I had somehow gotten on his radar. All I could hope for is that he would start with his question before I started blurting out confessions to whatever I think I did wrong just to get out of his presence.

"We received a report," he started, his words coming out slow, almost like he was picking his words carefully. Which was odd. I cocked my head to the side, my arms coming to cross over my chest as I waited to hear more about this report. Obviously, it had something to do with me, but what exactly?

"We received a report from a concerned citizen." He tapped at his notebook and I finally took in the police officer. His hazel eyes bore into me, a color that almost matched his skin tone, a line through his right eyebrow. Short dark brown hair on top of his head, but a whole lot more for a beard. His posture was slightly slouched over as he waited to write my confession in his notebook, but I knew he was taller than me. "Can you provide a comment?"

"I'm afraid I can't provide a comment unless I know what the report is about," I countered, unsure why he wasn't getting straight to the point.

"So you don't know?"

"I don't," I replied. This was eerily familiar to when someone would get pulled over by a cop and they would ask if the person knew why they had been pulled over. But I wasn't driving, and I didn't do anything that I knew of to warrant a visit from the police.

"The report…" He tapped at his notebook. "…said threats were exchanged."

"Huh, threats?" I repeated. An image of the man with blond hair that was glued to his head popped into my mind. That was the only person with an uncivil interaction. I frowned as my shoulders sagged. That had to be why he was here. "I think I know what you are talking about, but there weren't any threats exchanged on my part. It was all on the guy's side, Mr...?" I trailed off as I realized I hadn't gotten the police officer's name! With a quick squint and a tilt of my head, I could see that he wore a nametag.

"Erickson," I said, as I read the name.

"*Officer* Erickson to you."

"Officer Erickson," I corrected myself, trying to hide the grimace. "I can assure you everything was one sided when it came to threats."

"We will see about that," he said as he narrowed his eyes, his breathing stilling as he took me in before grinning. "I'll look into it." His voice came out light and comforting.

He was an odd one. One moment he acted like I was the culprit and the next like I was the victim. Hopefully, he could put aside whatever thoughts were running through his head to cause him to switch sides so suddenly and figure out what was going on with that crazed man.

I nodded. "Please do. I have nothing to hide." Other than I came from a long line of witches yet have no idea how to do magic, but that was small potatoes compared to what was going on.

Officer Erickson closed his notebook and shoved it back into his breast pocket before sliding the pen on it so it could hang freely. "My job is to keep the peace in our little cozy part of town." He clasped his hands together and cracked his knuckles. "Keep out of trouble. The last thing we need is a Wayward stirring up trouble." He positioned his hands on his belt as he gave me another grin.

"What does that mean?" I blurted, as I crossed my arms over my chest. What was up with everyone talking about Waywards like it was a bad omen to see one? First the man with blond hair and now a police officer? Was there going to be another one before the day ended?

"Have a good day, Ms. Wayward."

With a quick wave, grin still on his face, he turned on his heels and headed for the front door, only stopping once to run his finger across a shelf to inspect for dust before the bell above the door jingled, signaling his departure.

I waited till Officer Erickson to walk down the street and out of view before collapsing into my seat behind the counter. My foot knocked into the bucket of cleaning solution I had mixed together to help whip this place back into shape. I needed to stay focused and make sure there wasn't a speck of grime so the Wayward Shop of Mysteries could open for business while the officer solved whatever was happening outside.

Chapter 8

With my chest thrust out and my chin held high, I took in the front of the shop. The bookshelves sparkled. The amount of elbow grease needed to wipe those clean had been ridiculous. After Officer Erickson's display, I had done another once-over to make sure. Just in case, he came back to wipe his finger along the shelves once more.

"Not bad for a day of work," I said out loud, letting loose an appreciative whistle. I really had outdone myself with all the cleaning I had done. My gaze drifted towards the back room, where the cauldron and scattered boxes still laid covered in layers of abandonment. But that was for another time because right now it was time for a reward. A sweet one.

Quickly making my way out of the shop, closing the door behind me, and only briefly pausing at the street to check both ways, I crossed over to my destination. Night had already fallen, and the open sign on the bakery was unlit, but I knew Warren was still in there by the way his head would pop in and out of view.

I knocked against the locked door. His body jerked as he looked in my direction before smiling and waving.

"How did the day of cleaning go?" he asked as he unlocked the door and held it open for me, his own bell above the door jingling as I entered.

"Pretty well, if I say so. I got a lot of stuff done and I am one step closer to opening up," I said as I made my way over to the counter, where a light pink box was sitting tied up in an equally pink ribbon. "Thought the ribbons were a onetime thing?" I inquired as I picked up the little box to inspect it. Maybe April had picked out this one as well.

"For special occasions," he muttered, making his way to stand next to me. "It's for you. I was going to bring it over when I finished up here."

I untied the ribbon as I opened the pink box. The sweet aroma of warm apples greeted me as I sniffed the air, committing the scent to memory. Hesitantly, I picked up the sweet-smelling dessert. It was crisp but warm and gooey from the apples seeping through. Examining the little delight, it was easy to identify it as an apple turnover.

"You are the best!" I gushed as I took a bite of the sweet but hot piece of turnover, the crust breaking apart in my mouth as the apples warmed my mouth. "Are you still closing up?" The question came out muffled as I took another bite.

"Unfortunately. There are still a few more things I need to do in the kitchen before I can head home for the night." He let loose a sigh as he leaned on the counter. "But you are done for the night?"

I nodded.

"Well, don't wait for me. I'm sure we will see each other tomorrow. Neighbors and all." He chuckled as he rubbed at the back of his neck. I glanced outside, and it was dark. The extra cleaning I did because of Officer Erickson had me staying longer than I had intended, and the short detour for some sweets didn't help.

"You are right." I closed the pink box as I shifted towards the front door. "Thank you! You are seriously the best." And he was. He was feeding an addiction I didn't even know I had. Sweets was always a weakness of mine and there were plenty of shops to visit in New York to satisfy my sweet tooth. But I stayed away. My previous boyfriend had always reminded me that I was just a few pounds away from being overweight. Not anymore. I was going to enjoy everything and anything. Magical and sweet. "See you tomorrow."

I waved goodbye as I headed outside with a box of apple turnovers in hand. A soft audible click drew my attention as I saw Warren lock the door behind me and wave goodbye, watching me as I walked down the street.

There was a slight bounce in my step as I hurried home. All I wanted was to make a cup of tea, crack open a book, and devour the rest of the apple turnovers before calling it for the night. Forget about the days of dust scrubbing I had done and just think about the next step of opening the store to the public. Which meant the start of learning how to wield magic.

"Maybe?" I muttered as I examined my hand out in front of me, making sure not to drop my box of delights. It was always described that magic flowed with warmth, coursing through your body as if snuggled up in a blanket next to a fireplace. The comfort it provided was like a best friend where no words needed to be exchanged, just smiles.

I had been able to wield magic at one point in my life. It was very fleeting though. I remembered my grandma standing on her tippy toes as she stirred the contents of a spell in her cauldron as she sang out words to a spell she'd created. I had joined her, enthralled by her singing, and that was when I felt the warmness fill my body. She had screamed in delight when she noticed the magic. I frowned as I recalled her smile, forced as it didn't reach ear to ear, when I told her I was done with magic.

"Sorry it took me so long."

She couldn't hear me, but speaking it out loud helped. Everything was finally starting to fall into place in this new chapter of life. Magic would come. The warmth would course through my body as I created items to sell to the public. Just not now, as I went back to holding the box with two hands. The only warmth was coming from the pink container that held additional apple turnovers that were calling my name.

I froze, the warmth evaporating as dread filled my stomach, twisting it into knots as I stood in the middle of the sidewalk. I had been so lost in memory lane I hadn't noticed the streetlights were flickering. The path ahead felt like the end of the world as the light flicked in and out of existence. I couldn't help but chew on my bottom lip as I contemplated continuing to go home or head back and wait for Warren to finish up.

What is going on?

Nausea washed through my body and I wobbled, my vision blurring for a moment as I tightly closed my eyes, trying to get the world to be still. I took a step forward, the dread bubbling to fill my throat like I was drowning.

Was I supposed to not go home?

I turned back towards the shops, the knot in my stomach loosening as my breathing got better. I pursed my lips as I tossed a look over my shoulder. The lights behind me were still flickering, but the lights where I had come from were solid as could be. Unease teased at my senses as I waited in limbo, figuring out what I should do. I clutched the apple turnovers closer to my chest, almost squashing the box in an attempt to feel warmth. To have comfort.

I'm heading back.

There wasn't a bounce in my step due to happiness, more due to how creeped out I was. I hauled myself down the block, speed-walking back. Something was wrong, but I wasn't sure. I would just wait for Warren, then I could figure out what to do next. Maybe something was wrong with him and that was why I couldn't take another step away?

The dread bubbled back inside, but it wasn't as all-consuming as before. Just a little poke that let me know it was there and it wasn't going away just yet. Not till I figured out the source of why it had appeared.

Left.

Right.

Skip a few.

The bakery popped into view, the light still on, indicating Warren still hadn't finished up. I had almost picked up my pace to a run to confirm he was okay and to get some company when a dark blob across the street grabbed my attention, forcing me to a halt. Craning my neck, and squinting, I tried to make out the dark mess on the sidewalk. Normally, I would have ignored it. Not my monkey, not my business. But it was my business because it was on the front steps of the Wayward Shop of Mysteries. And it wasn't there when I left.

Walking slowly, I made my way over to Sweet Tokens of Sugar to peer through the window. Warren shuffled into the kitchen. He wouldn't be able to see me unless he stopped and looked up front, but he was in the zone. No doubt trying to finish up his tasks so he could go home.

"If Warren is in there, then who or what is..." I muttered as I turned to look across the street, pointing to the blob. "...that?" Surely, Warren didn't leave me another gift, but maybe he did? Was it something for the store? *But why leave it on the ground?*

I slowly crossed the street, the dread in my stomach evaporating as I got closer. So this was what I was meant to find and what had blocked me from going home. But what was it? Surely a gift would have more vibrant colors instead of being just a void.

"Hello?"

I had no idea if the creature was alive or not, man or beast. Better to be safe than sorry, just in case it turned out to be some random thing. But the object didn't move as I called out once more. Instantly, I checked off the possibility that it was alive.

I inched my way towards the blob on my doorstep, poking at it with my foot. It was squishy yet hard? Like it had a layer of something soft which covered something hard underneath it. So I poked it again, a little stronger as the blob flipped over, blond hair being exposed.

A scream almost ripped out my throat, but I managed to catch myself as I rolled my eyes at who it was.

"Sir, I know you don't like me, but I don't think it's wise to sleep here," I muttered as I poked the blond-haired man again. Why he thought yelling at me and then coming back to sleep in front of my door was a good idea was beyond me. Probably thought it was a good way to get a rise out of me. No doubt wanted to scare me, but he hadn't planned on me coming back, or had just missed me.

"Hello?" I spoke a little louder as I crouched to examine the guy. His eyes were closed, and his chest wasn't rising.

A normal alive person's chest would move, but his didn't. That feeling of dread returned and my mouth fell open.

"Is this a joke?" My words came out in a jumbled mess. "All this to get me to leave town?" Words fluttered out my mouth faster than I could process what was really unfolding in front of me. He wasn't alive. He was dead. I was next to a dead person.

Tears pricked at the corner of my eyes as I stood in denial. This was supposed to be a new chapter, one with wonderful magical things. Instead, I got a dead body.

Nothing good can happen with a Wayward back in town.

My legs shook as they gave out underneath me, my butt crashing to the pavement. My apple turnovers crashed to the ground as I just sat in silence, really soaking it in. This was really happening. With shaking hands, I pinched myself. A jolt coursed through me, but the body didn't disappear. It was here. So I did the only logical thing and screamed for help.

"WARREN!!!"

My voice carried on the wind, fueled by confusion but also shock. In the distance, I could hear the fierce jingle of a bell as Warren shouted my name.

"What's going on?" he asked. I watched him take everything in, his eyes going wide as he noticed the person next to me.

"Dead ... guy..." I muttered.

"What happened to him?" Warren asked quickly as he placed his fingers against the throat of the man. He had asked a question that I didn't have an answer to. A question that I would very much like to have answered myself. Yet I knew that the million-dollar question he asked was going to be answered soon, as the dread returned to the pit of my stomach.

Chapter 9

Once more I found myself on the receiving end of having to watch Officer Erickson scribble away in the little notebook of his that he seemed to always carry on him. When Warren had called reporting the dead body to the police, they had been prompt in showing up. Nothing like a dead body to get the police moving double speed. They also picked us up and put us in an interrogation room.

Officer Erickson tapped his pen on the table as he leaned back in his chair. "Tell me the story from the very beginning." I licked my lips as I tried to stay calm. It was late, I was tired, I had seen a dead body, and my mind was frazzled. I had already told my story and now he was asking for it again?

"Yes, again," he said as if reading my mind.

I had a feeling that I could state my side of the story a million times and he would still ask me to say it again. His way of trying to catch me in a lie, but there was no lie to tell. The words spilled from my mouth once more, the memory still fresh in my mind. I spoke about doing another once-over of the shop because he had dragged his finger along my shelves, making me self-conscious that there was still a layer of grime left. Then I talked about going home and stumbling upon a dead body in front of my shop.

"So let me get this straight, you left Sweet Tokens of Sugar to go home?" His tone came out questioningly, but I ignored it and nodded. I had said I did several times. "With a box of apple turnovers that you no longer have..."

I frowned. Why out of everything did he have to remind me of the sweet apply gooey dessert than been ruined?

"Yes, they got ruined when I stumbled upon the dead body."

"Uh huh..." he said as he chewed on his pen before pointing it in my direction. "But before that, the lights had flickered?"

"That's correct."

"Like in the movies?"

"I guess?" I countered.

"And you were filled with a sense of doom?"

"That is correct."

Officer Erickson raised his eyebrows as he gave me a pointed look. It sounded ridiculous, but it was the truth. It would make it a little more believable if I declared I was a witch and I think it was my witchy sixth sense coming to fruition, but I couldn't say that. He was already looking at me like a crazy person.

"Like a horror movie sixth sense where you're walking to your doom?" he pressed, his questioning getting more ridiculous as he grinned.

"I guess?" I answered again.

"And you turned back, and there was a dead guy right in front of your shop." He scribbled in his notebook, his grin still etched on his face. "Your shop out of all the shops on the block."

I crinkled my nose. It wasn't a question; it was phrased more like a statement. Like a matter of fact, but it wasn't like I asked him to die in front of my shop. I couldn't explain why he decided to drop dead there.

"And all of this happened after your altercation with the man...?" He trailed off, pointing his pen at me once more, his grin reaching from ear to ear as if he had caught me. But he hadn't because I had done nothing wrong. "Don't you find that a little odd?" He reached up to stroke his beard as he set the pen behind his ear.

"It is odd, but it's the truth."

"And that's the entire story?" he asked, tucking his notepad into his breast pocket.

"It hasn't changed from the last time I told it." My words came out blunter than I had expected. I had been doing my best to stay patient. He was solving a case after all, but having me repeat myself over and over was crazy.

"And yet something seems to be missing..." He said as he stood from his seat, crossing his arms as he looked down at me.

"You can talk to Warren. He was there. Our stories line up."

Officer Erickson smirked as he set both hands on the table to look into my eyes. "Line up, eh? How odd for you to use that phrase." He pulled back and made his way over to the door and jerked it open. "Don't worry, he's talking to a buddy of mine. We will see if your stories line up." He jerked his finger out the door to point to the hallway. "Well, Ms. Wayward, you are free to go."

"I am?" I blurted as I stood up, my metal chair screeching from the abrupt movement.

"Unless you got something else you would like to share? Maybe, how he died?"

"No idea," I blurted as I quickly made my way out of the interrogation room and turned down the hallway to bolt out of the police department so I could finally go home.

"Ms. Wayward," Officer Erickson called out to me as he poked his head out, a smirk still on his face. "Don't be leaving town until we find out more information." I nodded, but he held up his finger, indicating one moment. "If I find information linking you to this case, you can bet you will be back here." He waved me off. "Now have a good day, Ms. Wayward." Then the door slammed, leaving me in the hallway to retrace my steps out of the police building on my own.

With shoulders slouched and eyes trained on the ground, I did my best to not draw attention to myself. I was sure I looked tired, maybe smelled a little, but most of all I was trying to avoid having to tell my story for the millionth time in one night. Who knew starting a new chapter of my life would end up with me being questioned at a police station about a dead man who wanted me gone...

"Serafina!"

I perked up at my name being called. I looked around. A few officers sitting at desks or talking to others looked up in my direction briefly to see who had decided to shout while they worked.

"You were gone longer than I expected."

I turned around to come face to face with Warren. "You are still here as well?" I asked as I followed him.

"I was waiting for you. I wanted to make sure you were okay after..." He trailed off. He didn't need to say what he was thinking, because I knew. We both knew. "How are you?" he asked, his voice soft.

"Fine," I muttered. "Just tired. I really just want to go home," I added as I knew I had been short with just a one-word answer. Warren smiled as he beckoned me to follow him as we turned a corner, the front door popping into view. He pushed ahead to hold open the door.

Cold air blasted against my skin. I hadn't realized how warm it was in the station. Was that a tactic of theirs? Officer Erickson's words popping into my head, wishing me a good day. Night had passed, the sun was already creeping in and would be shining brightly in the sky soon. My entire night had been consumed with dealing with death and the police. Never in a million years did I think that was a way I could spend my night.

"Did you get bombarded with telling your story a million times?" I inquired as we started to walk down the street, away from the station.

"Nah, I'm a regular here so they know me."

I paused, taking a step back from Warren as my mouth dropped open, my eyebrows furrowing together.

"Not in that way!" he exclaimed, shaking his hands in the air as I gave him a pointed look. "I swear! I know several of the guys, we hang out often." Then Warren smiled. "Plus you know that stereotype about police and donuts?" He leaned in to whisper in my ear: "It's true."

A laugh erupted from within, making me feel light. It was a good change of topic, a nice distraction from all the talk of a dead guy. We continued down the street, putting distance between us and the station.

"Oh, by the way, if you want more apple turnovers I have a few extra at the shop." Warren let loose a light chuckle as he rubbed at the back of his neck. "Couldn't help but notice them on the ground when the police came by."

"That would be lovely," I replied as hastened our pace down the street towards Sweet Tokens of Sugar so I collect another box of the sweet warm delights. It was no longer night, but the great thing about sweets is that they could be enjoyed at all times.

We walked the rest of the way in silence. When arriving at his shop, Warren unlocked it and held the door open, the bell above the door chiming as we entered.

"How many would you like?" he inquired as he made his way around the counter.

"Two should be fine."

Internally, I felt like I should get more. All the comfort food in the world would be needed to keep my mind off the night's activities once I was alone.

"Alright, then," Warren replied as he shifted behind the counter to disappear into the kitchen. Noise emitted from the back as he got to work, putting together a small box of apple turnovers that I could take home. He was only gone a minute before he re-emerged with a blue box this time, no ribbon on it, and he thrust it in my direction. For some reason, I got the urge to take a peek at the contents. There weren't just two apple turnovers in there, but five warm apple delights squeezed in the small box.

"Figured you could use the pick-me-upper."

He had no idea how right he was.

Chapter 10

For some odd reason, I had decided to come into the shop even though just mere hours ago I was at the police station. Sleep had claimed me quickly when I got home thanks to one warm apple turnover and a snuggle between my sheets. But sleep didn't stay long, and now all I wanted to do now was go home and sleep some more, but I didn't even want to make the trip back home to do so.

"Afternoon, Ms. Wayward."

I closed my eyes, willing the person to go away and come back when I was a better mood, and most of all more awake. I nuzzled my head deeper into the crook of my arm as I hoped the person would think I was asleep and not hear. I didn't want to be rude to a potential customer, but surely they would have to cut me some slack. Not many people had to deal with a dead body.

"Ms. Wayward...?"

There would be no rest for me. I groaned, picking myself off the counter while mustering a small smile, only for it to vanish as I identified who had spoken. "Hello," I muttered, not bothering to stand up. I couldn't believe I hadn't recognized his voice, not after having to listen to it all night. Just more proof that I was too tired, and that dragging myself out of bed was a bad idea.

"I see you have been productive with your day."

I crinkled my nose. There was mirth in Officer Erickson's tone. A jab at him, catching me sleeping on the job: "It could have been more productive if I was allowed to go home earlier," I spit out, the crankiness of not getting more sleep already biting me in the butt. Upsetting Officer Erickson was one sure way to be hauled down to the station for more questioning. "What can I do for you?" Did he already find something about the death? If so, he worked fast.

Officer Erickson made his way over to stand in front of the counter, notepad still tucked into his breast pocket as he watched me. "We did manage to find a link between Mr. Isaac Cannon and your family."

"Who?" I blurted.

"The man that died on your front steps. Did you not remember his name?" He frowned, his arms crossing in front of his chest. As I looked up at him, I racked my brain trying to figure out if anyone had actually uttered the person's name. There was a chance he could have said it and I just didn't commit it to memory due to the shock of last night's event.

"Oh," I muttered, not wanting to provide any insight on the fact I truly had not remembered his name. "What is the connection?" I inquired, as I stood from my seat, still not putting me on the same level as the officer.

"It turns out Mr. Cannon's father had actually mugged your grandfather from a report I dug up."

I stood still, a cold shiver passing through me as I processed his words. The man now identified as Isaac Cannon had arrived at my shop threatening me like I had done something wrong. Like my family had wronged him in some way, but it had been the other way this whole time. "I didn't know that," I said as I stared at Officer Erickson in bewilderment. With every day that passed, I was encountering something weird with my new home.

"According to the report, only money was stolen. No expensive items." Officer Erickson stroked his beard. "It seems your grandfather wasn't one for flaunting his money."

Money? My grandparents never seemed like the type to have a bunch of money. They were frugal. What was the point of buying stuff when all it took was some elbow grease and magic to make a magical version that would last longer? Though that wasn't saying magical items were cheap; they could rack up an extremely high bill, depending on the item needed.

"There was something else in the report," Officer Erickson said, pulling me from my thoughts. I tilted my head to the side and waited for him to elaborate. Was there another altercation between our families?

"There was a note in the report."

"A note about what?"

"Something to do with a Wayward curse."

"A curse?" I repeated, unsure if I had heard him correctly. But he nodded, confirming that I hadn't mistaken the word *curse* from something else.

"Would you like to share information about your family, Ms. Wayward?"

About my family?

When I thought about my family, a few words popped into mind. *Big* for how large my extended family was. *Magical*, that was a given. *Curse*, though? It didn't pop into my head. I had never heard about a curse in my family.

It seems I might not know much about my family after all. All those years apart would do that.

I frowned as I dropped my shoulders. "Not sure what you are talking about," I replied, hoping he wouldn't press further. I had no information to share.

"Well, Ms. Wayward…" He pressed his lips together and raised an eyebrow as if waiting to see if I would offer something, but when I didn't speak he continued: "If you do manage to find something, don't hesitate at all to reach out." He grunted before turning swiftly on his heels to leave the shop. I watched him leave, the bell above the door chiming as he shot me one last look before walking down the street towards the station.

I waited for an extra three minutes to make sure he wasn't going to be popping back up before gripping fistfuls of my hair as I blabbered out loud to the empty shop: "Curses? Curses! I'm not qualified to deal with curses. I can barely do magic!" I plopped down in my seat and let loose a heavy sigh.

I was in over my head. There was no doubt about it. To think I could just move across the country and start learning magic after years of neglecting it was an oversight. The curses were the nail in the coffin that I had severely forgotten that magic wasn't something simple. It was complex with multiple layers, multiple specialties, and curses were real.

And now I had to figure out what was going on.

Chapter 11

When my stomach grumbled, pulling me from the rampaging thoughts in my mind, I wasted no time in leaving the shop and making my way down the street—in the opposite direction of the station, to decrease my chances of running into Officer Erickson.

Not wanting to dwell in my mind about magic and certainly not curses, I took in the other shops on the block. Next to the Wayward Shop of Mysteries was an empty building with a For Rent sign. There was a thin layer of grime in the place, nothing compared to what had greeted me, meaning this place had been vacant for a little but not a long time.

"Maybe if the business goes well, I can expand?" I said as I peered through the glass window. In order to expand, I had to learn magic. Which was a lot easier said than done. I couldn't help but let loose another sigh. Everything revolved around magic. Eventually I would have to rip the Band-Aid off and just do the magic, but I had to finish cleaning up first.

Grrr.

"Okay, okay..." I muttered as I patted my stomach to quiet the sounds it was making. My dinner had comprised of an apple turnover, and my breakfast had consisted of the same thing. It was time I finally got some food in me before I collapsed and joined Isaac Cannon on the other side.

Wind brushed against my exposed skin, carrying a sweet smell. Sticking my nose up in the air, I sniffed, trying to figure out exactly was so alluring. It wasn't sweet like sugary sweet like from the bakery. More like a savory aroma of something toasted that smelled wonderful. So wonderful that my stomach grumbled once more. I started down the street again, nose slightly up like a bloodhound as I tried to track down what was hypnotizing me.

Huh?

I paused at a flower shop as a lady inside waved enthusiastically. I pointed to myself to see if she was trying to grab my attention as she nodded and held up a vase of flowers and thrust in my direction, her head nodding rapidly.

"No, thanks!" I yelled as I rushed past the shop before the flower lady could walk outside and try to get me to come in and buy something. Slowing down to a stroll, laughter filled the air from across the street: a wide-open park with kids running wild, screaming and laughing as they chased one another. A row of parents were sitting at the benches watching them.

Food can wait, I thought as I paused and watched the kids. So filled with joy, unaware of what was going on in the world. *Of what happened just last night, only a few shops down*. It must be nice to just enjoy and not worry. A memory of my grandfather popped in my mind as he would take out of the shop while grandma worked in the back brewing something in her cauldron. He had liked to joke that if I stood over the cauldron long enough, inhaling all the smoke that would spill over the rim, eventually I would turn into a crazy witch like my grandma. My cheeks hurt as my smile grew. He always liked to make fun of her, teasing that witches who inhaled too much smoke would turn green and become a wicked witch. Only grandma never thought it was funny, throwing whatever happened to be in her hand at his head if she overheard him. That's why he liked to take me to the park, an excuse to escape her wrath after he decided to push her buttons.

My attention shifted from the children to a group of adults who were looking at me and pointing. Instantly, I turned on my heels and started down the street with my head down, hoping my hair covered all of my face so they couldn't identify me. I hadn't been staring, just lost in memory lane. The savory aroma that smelled an awful lot like cheese was stronger. I was getting closer. I picked up my pace, once more sniffing the air as I tried to locate the source.

A jingle of a door opening grabbed my attention, so I sidestepped from knocking into the man walking backwards out of a pizza shop with several boxes in his arms.

"Sorry!" he called as he tossed a look over his shoulder at me before rushing down the street in the direction I had just come from. The smell that followed him smelled like toasted cheese, but not exactly what was drawing my attention.

"Welcome to Stuffed Sub Shop, the site where we satisfy all your stuffed sub needs!" a man exclaimed as he pushed open the door to the shop right next door to the pizza place.

"Uh," I replied, surprised by his sudden appearance. He had a huge smile on his face, his black hair pulled back into a man bun as he wore a white button-down shirt with a white apron.

"What can we get for you today, ma'am?" he asked as he held the door open, his gray eyes twinkling as he blocked my path, leaving me with the choice of walking into the shop or being rude. "We got cold subs, hot subs, and we can even do warm subs if you fancy!"

Warm subs?

What on Earth classified as a warm sub? That was something I didn't want to find out. "Maybe just a cold sub? Nothing too ... fancy, please."

"Would you like that extra stuffed? One hundred percent satisfaction guaranteed!" he exclaimed as he made his way behind the counter.

"Sure?" I hadn't eaten a lot today and the extra food might actually work in my favor. He was just too bubbly of a person that I felt odd saying no to him.

"Alright, then!" he chirped as he grabbed a piece of bread. "One cold sub extra stuffed coming right up!" and got to work making my food. As he got to work, my mouth dropped lower and lower. When he meant extra stuffed, I had thought maybe double at most. It wasn't double. Double was a long time ago, and he kept going. Packing it down before piling some more until he squished the bread together in an attempt to get the sub to close.

"One hundred percent satisfaction guaranteed!"

There was no doubt about that.

Chapter 12

"**I**'m full ... but maybe one more?" I mumbled as I squeezed the pieces of the bread together in order to shove the overstuffed sub into my mouth. Did Stuffed Sub Shop go overkill with how stuffed their food was? *Absolutely.* Would I be going back there for another sub? Absolutely *yes*, no doubt about it. One hundred percent satisfaction guaranteed, indeed. Somehow managing to swallow the last of bite of the sub, I leaned back in my seat, rubbing my stomach, trying to smooth away the ache before it could creep in. Only half the sub had been devoured, the other half still lay on the table waiting for me. But that would be for another time.

With no food to occupy my thoughts, it left me alone to ponder about what to do next with the shop. Eventually, I would have to make my way into the back room and clean up there. Just thinking about the additional cleaning made me depressed, when instead I could think about how to style the front.

Hmmm..

I took in the Wayward Shop of Mysteries and imagined what it would look like once the shelves were filled with products. The bookcases were all some type of natural wood, not all the same tone but close enough that it blended. Yet this was a new chapter, which meant out with the old and in with the new? I frowned as I rested my elbows on the counter, my head in my hands as I gazed around the shop again. Painting things white was very in style, something I liked because it looked clean. Then again, there was just something about the rustic feel of having the natural wood shine through. Just another thing to add to my long list of things to do for the shop. I reached for the other half of my sub, wrapping it up, and a few pieces of food fell to the ground from how stuffed it was. As I bent down to clean up my mess, I paused, frozen from the words that drifted into the shop.

Why did I leave the door propped open?

"Did you hear there is a Wayward back in town?" a female said as I stayed bent behind the counter. Part of me wanted to burst up and let them know I was here. But the part that won out was staying hidden to listen to what they had to say about me. I'd only been here a few days and I was the hot topic of Snowton Heights.

"I heard!" another female said. This time it was a higher pitch.

"You know what they are saying ... with a Wayward back in town, the curse is back," the first lady chimed in, her voice taking on a spooky tone towards the end. My chest grew heavy. Starting over would be hard with a curse hanging over my head.

"Oh, stop that!" the second girl chimed in, letting loose a round of giggles, "it doesn't work like that!"

"And how would you know? There has already been a dead body since her arrival."

My heart dropped. Did they think it was because of me that he died?

"No way! You have to be kidding!" the second female said, the mirth in her tone gone.

"Nope, he died right here," the first female said, no doubt pointing to the spot where there had been a dead body just last night. "Should we go inside and see what she looks like?"

"Absolutely not! We have to get out of here!"

I stayed bent behind the counter as I heard their voices grow distant. I still didn't want to get up and expose myself just in case I'd heard wrong and set myself up to be judged by them on something I knew nothing about.

When several minutes had passed, I picked up the scrap of food off the floor and threw it in the trash, making sure to close the door so no more unwanted conversations would filter through.

I paced the shop. "Was this a mistake?" I mumbled as I gripped my chin, my pacing never stopping. "Should I go back to New York?" I shook my head, removing those thoughts. That option wasn't even an option. I had no job and nowhere to stay if I ventured back into the city, unless I moved in with my parents. Now that had me pausing as I mulled over what I had said.

Move.

Back.

Home.

Vigorously, I shook that thought from my head. There was no way I was going back home unless it was absolutely the last option available. There was just no way I could live back at home with my parents. I wanted to explore magic on my own, at a slow pace instead of being drowned in their smothering. Which left me with only one option.

Figure out what happened to Isaac Cannon while some-how figuring out what curse everyone was talking about. Solving one thing sounded hard, but figuring out both? I was about to be in for a wild ride.

Chapter 13

"How is the cleaning going?" Warren asked as he walked up and down the shop inspecting the bookcases. Thankfully, he wasn't like Officer Erickson, who had run his finger up and down the shelves to inspect it for grime. I don't think I could have handled another cleaning when there was already more to do.

"Still have the back to do, but I should be done soon." *Hopefully.* It all depended on how much of my time would be taken up with solving Isaac Cannon's death and figuring out what curse my family had a play in.

"I can't wait to see what you do with this place," Warren said as he rubbed at the back of his neck, his lips curving into a smile. "I'll make sure to be your very first customer!"

If I managed to open the shop. At the rate hurdles were being thrown in my path, there was no finish line in sight. My shoulders sagged at the thought. The townsfolk probably wanted to run me out of business rather than support me when I opened.

Warren pulled a bag from his side and he set it on the counter, drawing my attention. It wasn't his usual box of treats that I was starting to think was his signature.

"Hope you are in a sweet mood." He smiled as he let loose a small chuckle before pulling down the edge of the bag to expose its contents. "Brought over some raspberry macaroons for you to try."

"At this rate, you are trying to sweeten me up and fatten me up," I joked as I grabbed the raspberry treat he held out for me.

"Maybe next time I'll bring a drink too." Warren raised his macaroon in the air, thrust it in my direction, and smacked it against my own before biting into it. I followed suit.

"Once everything is open, we can celebrate."

"Sounds like a deal," Warren said, finishing off his macaroon with another bite. "Just to let you know, I signed you up to taste-test any future stuff I create." He let loose a chuckle. I was starting to realize that was a signature of his.

"I would have volunteered if I had known there was a list," I jokingly replied as I finished the raspberry treat he had brought over. "Warren.," I started as I licked my lips. While I would love to just sit back and relax, there was something I had to do before my time in Snowton Heights was cut short. "Do you know anything about the guy who died?"

"You mean Isaac Cannon?"

I nodded.

"From what I understand, the rest of his family had already passed on, and it's just him left now."

My heart was heavy hearing those words. My time with Isaac Cannon was short and unpleasant, but it didn't mean I couldn't feel bad for what he must have gone through. I bit my lip as I thought about my own family. If something were to happen tomorrow and one of my sisters died, I would regret it. Maybe I should pick up the phone and call them...

"Why ask about him?" Warren chimed in, cutting my somber thoughts short.

"Because I'm..." I started as I trailed off. Did I want to bring Warren in on my decision to look into Isaac Cannon and the curse everyone was talking about? He stared at me with his green eyes and I shook my head no. He was already super friendly and helpful, something I was grateful for, but I couldn't drag him into this. At least not yet. "Oh, do you know if he had a job, maybe a hobby or anything, to give me an idea about who he was?"

Warren raised his eyebrow, catching on to my change in topic, and gave me a quizzical look. "Well, he does stop by the bakery from time to time. Or did." Warren rubbed at the back of his neck. "He never mentioned a new job, so not sure about that part. But for hobbies? Hats."

"Hats? Like he collects them?"

"Everything about hats. He could go on and on about them if they ever came up in a conversation."

My time with Isaac Cannon was short, and most of that time was spent receiving threats from the man so it was kind of hard to believe he had a normal obsession with hats. They weren't crazy, and they weren't dangerous. But it was such a common item that I was afraid there would be nothing unique about it to help me figure out what had really happened to the man.

"Does that help?" Warren asked and I shrugged slightly.

"Possibly, I will have to look into it."

Warren gave me a look, a question dancing in his eyes, eyebrows drawn in, as he placed his hand on mine, my heart skipping a beat. "You know," he started as his other hand reached back to rub at his neck, "it's not your responsibility to look into his death just because he died in front of your shop."

Warren was right, it wasn't my responsibility, it was up to the police to figure out what had happened to the man. But Warren also wasn't there when I first met Isaac Cannon, and I knew there was something I had to uncover. Or at the very least figure out what this Wayward curse was. Because it wasn't something just a dead man talked about, those still living knew, and I wanted any chance to have a new beginning here. I would have to look into it.

There weren't a lot of people I could reach out to in town to figure out more about the man's past. I pursed my lips; I could always go back and ask Officer Erickson, but I knew that wasn't such a good idea. He was still looking into me to figure out my connection to the man, and if I showed up having significantly higher interest he would be alarmed. Instead, I needed someone from the past who could tell me. Or some*thing* from the past.

"I have a few errands to run, so I have to head out," I said, smiling.

Warren nodded, tying off the bag of sweets, leaving it on the counter before he waved goodbye and left the shop. I was glad he didn't ask more questions or try to tell me again it wasn't my responsibility. When Warren had walked back into his store, I left the Wayward Shop of Mysteries, but not before locking up.

Already knowing the way, I headed down the block towards the library. It was a nice day out; I soaked in the sunlight that bathed the street. Several shops had their doors open, letting in the cool breeze. Laughter filled the air once more as I passed by the park. This time I didn't stop and get lost in memory lane. Hiding my face, I sped past the Stuffed Sub Shop to avoid being dragged back into the place—I still had food left over from last time. People passed me on the street, no one really stopping by to say hi or greet me, but I wasn't surprised. It was the Seattle cold that I was used to growing up with. Once people got familiar with me in town, there was no doubt I would be stopped to have conversations on the street.

I made my way down the street until the library popped into view, then I slowed down, a memory popping into my mind of my grandparents taking me here to read fantasy books. It was a way for them to try to spark the magic inside of me since I wasn't drawn to it in real life. Swallowing down the lump that had formed in my throat, I made my way up the steps of the library to enter the building. Directly in front of me upon entering the building was a lounge area, and just a few steps behind it were a set of elevators. On the right was a used book shop, and if I took the elevator up it would take me to the library portion of the building, but it was what was on the left that drew my attention: a computer lab.

"Library card?" the lady sitting behind the counter in the computer room asked as I entered. She placed her bookmark in her book and pushed up her glasses that had fallen to the tip of her nose before looking up at me.

"I'm new in town."

"In order to use the computers, you must have a library card."

"Okay, would it be possible to sign up for one now?" I inquired. I needed to get on those computers in order to do some research.

"Upstairs in the library." She pointed up to the ceiling before she popped open her book once more. I muttered a quick thanks before leaving the girl alone with her book and heading over to the elevator.

"Excuse me," I whispered to the first person who looked like they worked at the library once the elevator doors opened. "Can I register for a card, please?"

The lady behind the counter smiled and slid a piece of paper across the counter, followed by a pen. Quickly scribbling down my information, which took a moment to remember since I had new addresses now, I returned the information back to her. In less than a minute, I had a Snowton Heights library card and was making my way back down the elevator to the computer room. The lady, still reading her book, held up her hand for my card, before swiping it and returning it.

"All set."

Finally, I could get started on research on what really had happened here in the past in this not-so-cozy town. My fingers hovered above the keyboard as I debated on starting with researching the Wayward curse or about the Cannon family. So I closed my eyes and let my fingers move across the keyboard. My last name followed by the word *curse* populated in the search bar as I hit enter and waited, holding my breath. The screen flashed as article upon article popped up, all relating to the Wayward curse. My heart sank at seeing all the information. This wasn't just something a few people in town would know; every single person had to know about this! I sank in my chair at the realization that having a fresh start was no longer possible.

A WAYWARD BACK IN TOWN?

Well, that would explain why people had started showing up at the shop. An article published just a few days popped up in the most recent articles. It had announced to the whole world that I was here in Snowton Heights. A part of me wanted to click on it to see what they could have written about me without actually knowing me, but I passed. There was already enough bad news to deal with; I didn't want to pile on. Plus, I was already hearing what people thought. No reason to read about it too.

SNOWTON HEIGHTS OVERCOME WITH THE WAYWARD CURSE

Now that was a headline that caused me to crinkle my nose and do a double take. It was an extremely dramatic title; that would have invoked paranoia in the public. I could understand why Isaac Cannon acted the way he did if he thought I was bringing the curse back. But surely it couldn't be that bad? Not *plague* bad; if that were the case, I would have been run out of town before I could get settled.

Getting straight to the point, I clicked on the article and read over the contents. It seemed that after the mugging of my grandfather by Mr. Cannon's father, three additional families along with the Cannons came forward to claim they had been cursed by my family in retaliation. The first family that took up the bulk of the article was the Cannon family themselves. They had accused my family of cursing them, which forced them to shut down their business. Several lengthy quotes from the father were featured, but I skipped over them. The next person who came forward was Sarah Alma, who still attempted to do tarot readings despite having her business shut down. It was her comment that I read, a smile forming at how opposite her comment was. She had accused my grandparents of being fake witches, and they were trying to run her out of town because she was a true witch.

If only she knew...

The next family impacted, the Dunlap family, ran a restaurant they had to shut down in the middle of their rising popularity. And there was mention of another final family, but it was only two lines—no information provided about who that family could be and what type of business they'd had in Snowton Heights, only that they had lost millions due to this Wayward curse.

Cannon ... Alma ... Dunlap ... Mysterious family.

I scanned over the article once more, committing the names of the family to memory. Someone from one of those families would know more about the Wayward curse, and hopefully the Cannon family as well, due to their shared history of being supposed victims of my family.

"Excuse me?" I called out to the librarian, who was walking by. "Do I have any free prints to use?"

"One hundred pages per month for black and white. Ten cents a page for color," she answered before continuing to roll her cart down the aisle.

I nodded in thanks as I hit the print button on the computer. It was better to take the article with me as a reference and, of course, just in case I forgot. With it only being ten pages, it left enough in my print bucket if I needed to come back.

Chapter 14

Back at home, I stared at the papers in front of me on the counter. After the library, I had opted to go home and relax, fully intent on starting the next day on the right foot by being productive and looking into the families. The only thing I didn't know was how to locate them or how all of this was connected. I placed my elbow on the counter as I rested my head in my hand and let loose a big sigh. Somehow, all of this would come together.

"Are you open for business yet?"

I looked up at a man who had walked into the shop. He had his hands stuffed into the pockets of his white slacks, wearing a white button-down shirt that exposed a bit too much of his chest, with a gold chain on display.

"Not yet," I replied as I waved around the shop. "Still working on creating some products."

Despite my reply, he continued his stroll through the shop, browsing the shelves despite there being nothing to look at. Unless he was looking at air, because there was no grime to be found on my cases after all the cleaning I did.

"Can I help you?" I called, tilting my head to the side at his weird behavior.

"No, just stopping by."

"All right...?" I mumbled, still confused. But it wouldn't be the first time I'd encountered someone weird since coming to Snowton Heights. All I could hope for was that he also didn't end up dead in front of my door. The man popped into view and I took a moment to examine him some more. A slight clash to his pristine look was that he wore a pair of dark shades that made it impossible to identify his eye color. He had his equally dark hair slicked back, with some stubble growing on his chin.

"Doing some research?" he inquired as I looked down at my papers briefly. Even though it was extremely odd to be walking around an empty shop that had nothing to sell, I didn't want to kick the man out. There were already enough rumors going around about me. No reason to add being rude to the growing list.

"I guess I am," I replied as I leaned back in my chair as the man came to a stop before the counter I was at. With no invitation, and with the comfort of being at home, he sat on the counter, propping one leg up on it and looking down at me. I could only guess that his eyes were boring into me, unblinking, but I couldn't confirm that, not with the sunglasses he wore. Since he had already invited himself to sit on my counter, he invited himself to my stack of papers as well and he leafed through them.

"Excuse me?" I muttered, completely gobsmacked by this man I had never met before.

"You know," he started as he leaned one arm on his propped leg. "You won't get much from an ancient article. You need to talk to the actual people."

I furrowed my eyebrows in surprise as I took in this mysterious man. Who was he? He held out the papers to me. I grabbed them and set them back on the counter, this time out of the man's reach. His lips curved into a smirk, causing me to shiver. I had no idea who he was, but I knew I didn't want to stay in his presence for long.

"Thanks..." *I guess?* "I will make sure to do that." I had already planned on doing that.

"Well, you can start with me."

An audible gasp escaped as my mouth dropped open. Start with him? Who exactly was he? Was he someone mentioned in the article?

Cannon ... Alma ... Dunlap ... Mysterious family.

When I stayed silent, he pushed off my counter, shoving his hands back into his pockets. "Whatever you think happened recently or in the past, I and my family had nothing to do with. Don't go searching about my family."

"Who are you?" I whispered, slightly afraid of the mysterious man. His grin never left his face as he tipped his head, grabbed the stack of papers once more, before pointing to the brief passage about the unnamed family. Passing it in front of me, I glanced down to see what family he had come from, and it turned out to be the one most matching to the mysterious man because he came from the mysterious family that lost millions. Before I could question him some more about who exactly his family was or what his name was, he turned on his heels and headed towards the front door.

"Wait!" I shouted as I jumped from my chair to stop him from leaving. He had answers I desperately needed.

"I was at the charity event with my wife the night Mr. Cannon died."

I froze, forced to just watch him leave. Did I suspect foul play in Mr. Cannon's death? Not exactly, but now I was sure something had happened to the man. Why else would he make that comment when my article was about the Wayward curse? He knew they were linked, but the question was how? The bell above the door jingled as he made his grand escape down the block and out of sight, leaving me to collapse in my chair from the weight of what might be going on. This wasn't just about a curse, or the death of a man. There was something bigger going on, and I was in the thick of it.

Since the man had only left me with more questions, I would need to find a way to find answers. As I relaxed in my chair, I looked across the street to the bakery and smiled. While most people in Snowton Heights were playing a mysterious game, there was one person who had been nothing but helpful since my arrival. Grabbing a hold of the stack of papers, I bolted out of the shop and across the street to seek advice from Warren.

Chapter 15

"Hi, Serafina, I'll be with you in just one moment," Warren said as he did a small wave in my direction before returning to help the tall brunette man standing on the opposite side of the counter put several bags of sand tart cookies into a larger one. Warren didn't lie when he said those were the best sellers of his bakery.

"There you go, Adam, you are all set!"

"Thanks, I really appreciate it," Adam said as he grabbed the bag of cookies. "It helps me score brownie points in class." Both men let loose a round of laughter before Adam turned to leave the bakery.

"Oh, by the way, Adam!" Warren called out, causing the other man to pause and toss a look over his shoulder. "When is Erica going to become Mrs. Dunlap?"

I took in the brunette man. His name was Adam Dunlap? That was one of the names from the article of families who had been impacted by the Wayward curse.

"I want to get a good-paying job first before that."

Adam turned towards the door, his hand just brushing against the frame to push it open before I called out to him, stopping him in his tracks once more. I couldn't lose this opportunity to meet another person affected by the Wayward curse. Hopefully, he would be more open to talking than the last person.

"Wait! Did I hear correctly that your last name is Dunlap?"

"Adam Dunlap," he introduced himself, holding out his hand in my direction.

"Serafina Wayward," I replied as I shook his hand. "By chance, is this the same Dunlap family impacted by the Wayward curse?"

He raised his eyebrow, and cast a look over to Warren before settling on me once more. "I guess your last name explains the question. But yes, same Dunlap family. What can I do for you?" he asked as he looked at his watch, shifting his bag of sweets up his arm. Taking this moment,

I examined him from head to toe. Like the mysterious man, Adam was also wearing white. But instead of wearing fancy slacks and an unbuttoned shirt, he wore simple slacks with a chef's coat. The only thing missing from his outfit was a chef's hat; otherwise he would complete the image of someone who runs the kitchen as a chef.

"I'm doing some research on the Wayward curse," I started, a little hesitant to bring up the death of Isaac Cannon as well. The way the mysterious man had brought it up made it seem like something else was going on and that could mean foul play. Which meant I shouldn't give away too much information to Adam Dunlap till I could figure out if he had a play in what had happened.

"Research?" He looked at his watch once more before frowning. "That may take up more time than I thought..." he mumbled as he cast a glance over to the door. "Sorry, but I have class. Maybe another day?" He didn't wait for me to answer; he pushed open the door and stepped outside. "It was great meeting you though, Serafina!" he called out before the door shut and he speed-walked down the block and out of sight.

I stood standing still, pondering on his great escape. Did I phrase something wrong and tip him off? Or was he truly just busy and couldn't spare the extra few minutes?

"Researching the Wayward curse?"

I turned towards Warren, placing my papers on the counter in front of him so he could look. He wasted no time in reviewing them.

"I'm trying to ask family members about why they think they were cursed."

"Uh huh," he said as he sat the papers down. I reached for a pen on the counter and scribbled *a charity event* near the mysterious family and wrote *class* next to Dunlap. Going off the information I had left me with no idea how things connected. I would need to figure out some more information before things started to click.

"What's this about the charity event?" Warren asked as he pointed to my freshly written note.

"Some man came into the shop and said he was at a charity event the night of Isaac Cannon's death and then he vanished." I pouted as I used my hands to mimic something vanishing into thin air. "No other details. Don't even know his name."

"Well..." Warren started as he rubbed at the back of his neck, "there has only been one charity even recently, and it was held at the nightclub."

Grabbing the pen once more, I wrote *the nightclub* under charity event. It still didn't explain what was going on, but at least I had a location of where the mysterious man was.

"Now all that is left is the Alma family. By chance..." I started, but trailed off as Warren smiled.

"By chance do I know someone with the last name Alma?" he asked, and I nodded my head. He might not have magical powers, but he could read my mind.

"Let me see ... Alma ... Alma ... Alma..." he said, as he tapped at his chin, before sticking his finger up in the air in an ah-ha moment. "Sara Alma!"

"Sarah Alma is still alive?" I asked, puzzled.

"Why wouldn't she be?" He gave me a quizzical look before grabbing the papers once more, leafing through them till he pointed out the section of the article that mentioned the Alma family.

"Ohh. This is Sarah Alma with an H. I'm talking about Sara, as in S-A-R-A. Sara is the events coordinator at the nightclub." Warren slid the papers back across the counter so I could look at them. "They place orders with me quite often, but it's usually under the nightclub's name. That's why it took me a minute to figure out if I had heard that name before."

"Do you know where I can find Sara without the h?" I asked, with a smile. If Warren hadn't caught on that we were talking about a Sarah and a Sara, we would have gone back and forth confused as can be.

"Check the nightclub. If she isn't there, then I'm not sure."

"Thanks! I'll check it out." I grabbed my papers and headed towards the front door. "Thank you, Warren! You have been really helpful!"

"Wait! Grab some sand tarts." Warren rushed out from behind the counter, placing a small bag of sand tarts in my hand before opening the bakery door. "Glad I could help. Let me know if you need anything else, okay?"

"Will do!" With a wave goodbye, I made my way down the street towards the nightclub. I had passed it on the way to the police station, after all.

Chapter 16

I peered into the windows of the nightclub, though it was hard with the tint on it. Not being able to see if anyone was moving inside, I decided to see if the place was open. Night clubs were called *night* clubs for a reason, and that was because they were opened at *night*, and it was only midday. To my surprise, I discovered the door was unlocked.

"Hello?" I called as I stepped into the extremely lit building. A neon sign above an empty ticket station read Eclipse Club in vibrant flashing lights. With no one in immediate sight, I continued past the ticket station to where the fun would happen if this place were open. Several people walked about, some with boxes in their hands, others with cleaning supplies as they got to work, making the place spotless before they opened to the public. Hopefully, they wouldn't be too upset that I had invited myself in, but that seemed to be a common thing with how often it had happened to me.

"Excuse me?" I asked the person mopping the floor. He gave me a quick eye roll as he brushed back his black hair and leaned on his mop.

"We aren't open yet."

"I'm here to see Sara Alma," I replied.

He looked at me from head to toe before letting loose a heavy sigh, jerking a thumb over his shoulder to the steps behind him. "Upstairs office."

"Thank you," I muttered as the man wasted no time in returning to mopping the floor. With no one else stopping to ask me why I was here before they opened, I bounded up the steps. With no idea what Sara looked like, I would just have to hope she was the only person up here and I wouldn't have to go poking into the several offices situated on the second floor that I could see. The man mopping hadn't told me which office Sara was in, and there were three office doors up here. The light was on in the first one, so I knocked on the cherry wood.

"Come in!" a female voice said, so I pushed the door open and poked my head inside.

"By chance are you Sara Alma?" I inquired as I observed a female hunched over her desk, scribbling away in a journal. She had long brunette hair pulled back into a tight low ponytail, and wore a bright pink shirt.

"I am," she replied without looking up.

With confirmation that I had found the correct person, I fully stepped into her office. Sara ignored my presence as I strolled forward to sit in the chair in front of her desk. Even the screech of the wooden legs against the wood wasn't enough to draw her attention away from what she was working on.

"Um…" I started. Her pen slammed against her desk, her journal snapping closed. She gave me a look like she wanted to be anywhere but here.

"What do you need?" she barked as she opened a drawer and dropped her journal in it, leaning back in her chair, arms crossing over her chest. "You don't work here."

"I don't. But I'm looking into the Wayward curse. Do you know about it?"

She let loose a snort, followed by several short snorts in quick succession as her eyebrows raised. "Do I know about it? Is this a joke?"

"No," I replied, pursing my lips. She was definitely the most vocal of the people I had met, other than Isaac Cannon. Hopefully, this meant she would be willing to provide more information than Dunlap and the mysterious man. "I'm doing research on it, and your family was mentioned."

"Uh huh." She rolled her eyes as she tossed her ponytail over her shoulder. "And why would you be doing research on that?"

I paused, taking in Sara Alma. She was older, but it was hard to tell exactly how old she was because of the multiple layers of makeup she wore. In her attempt to hide her age, she had applied a hundred layers too much. Her green eyes bore into me, her face never losing the half amused and half annoyed expression she wore.

"Well, my name is Serafina Wayward," I answered, waiting for the shoe to drop. Dunlap had made a comment that it made sense a Wayward was looking into the Wayward curse, but he had acted civil. I wasn't too sure the lady before me would do the same.

"Ah..." Her expressive face morphed into one concealing all emotion. A knot twisted in my stomach at her sudden change in mood. Her lips pressed into a thin line, eyes focusing on something, just not me. "I see ... and what questions do you have?"

Ignoring the feeling of paranoia in my stomach, I took a deep breath and answered her: "Do you happen to know Isaac Cannon as well?"

There was a spark of emotion on her face, but just as quickly as it had popped up, it had disappeared.

"I do..." She leaned forward, her arms no longer crossed over her chest as she gripped on to the edges of her desk, "If you are trying to pin something on me, I was at the charity event making sure everything was running smoothly."

Just like the mysterious man.

Both of them had provided alibis so quickly, without even being prompted. There was something fishy going on and this just confirmed it. Isaac Cannon just didn't flop over dead on my front steps. Something had happened to him. But I couldn't accuse her—or the mysterious man, for that fact. I needed more information before I went about starting a witch hunt. Those never turned out well for the intended parties.

"That wasn't what I was going to ask."

"Then please see yourself out. I have things to do."

Sara turned to the laptop on her desk and began to type away. Her fingers blasting against the keyboard had me making a quick escape. The way she was pounding on those keys sounded like they would break very soon. And once they broke, she would need to direct her attention elsewhere, and I wanted to be nowhere near her. But she had provided more information, and now all I needed to do was connect the dots.

Chapter 17

Somehow I found myself back at Sweet Tokens of Sugar with a macaroon in one hand and papers in the other. At this point, I was spending more time over here on this side of the street than my side in the shop I was supposed to be opening. There was just something about this place. It could be the sweet aroma, the welcoming feeling, or the company. Whatever it was, I couldn't resist coming over to spend time in the bakery.

"Any luck connecting the dots?" Warren asked as he made his way over to the table I was sitting at. He had two cups of hot tea in hand, setting them down on the table before pulling out his chair and joining me.

"No sweets for you?" I asked as I grabbed the offered cup of tea.

Warren shook his head no, scratching at the back of his neck. "I had my fill already. Sometimes it's more fun seeing others enjoying my creations than eating them myself."

It made sense. I wasn't quite there to relish in the joy of others enjoying my products, as I still needed to create some items. But before I could do that, I had more pressing things to figure out. Namely, what happened to Isaac Cannon and the truth behind the Wayward curse. I couldn't help but let loose a deep sigh as I set the article down on the table. It contained additional scribbles on it as I wrote everything I had learned about the families.

"The curse is their connection but something is off..." I took a bite of my macaroon, talking with my mouth full. "Something is missing."

"What do you think it could be?" Warren asked as he took a sip of his tea, leaning in to peer at the papers. I joined him, scanning the article to see if anything would pop out. But it had to be the hundredth time I had read them. All of it was the same. All of it was blurring together, and no lines were forming.

"I'm not sure. I guess I had to do some additional research."

"And how do you expect to do that?"

I mulled over Warren's question. That was a very good question. One I didn't have the answer to but somehow needed to find quickly. Leaning back in my chair, I took another sip of my hot tea as I thought of my options.

"The mysterious man is out of the question right now. Can't exactly question someone if I don't know what their name is." Wearing all white with a gold chain wasn't a distinguishable enough outfit that it would be easy to identify where he worked, or where he had come from. But then I remembered how I felt around him and I wasn't too sure I wanted to be in his presence. Why did all of this have to be so difficult?

Warren nodded as he took another sip of his tea. "Alma isn't in the best mood to talk to me," I said, "and it would be hard to talk to her with the nightclub about to open. Then Dunlap is in class..." The only family left was the Cannon family, but they were all dead. And talking to the dead was advanced magic, and even then you had to have a knack for it.

"Since you are stuck, take some time to rest. Look over your notes with a fresh mind after you take some time away from it."

"Thanks, Warren," I responded as I picked up my hot tea and notes. "Don't know what I would do without you. I'll bring the teacup back tomorrow, if that's okay."

He shot a smile in my direction, giving me a thumbs-up as he watched me leave his bakery. I stared at my shop across the street. I didn't want to go back there even though I had work to do. Work that would all be pointless if I couldn't figure out how everything connected together. Rolling up the papers, I stuffed them under my arm as I took another sip of my tea and started on the walk home.

Cars buzzing by, people muttering to each other, and the occasional bark from a dog filled the air with noise, providing comfort from all the thoughts running rampant in my mind. Along with the noise, fresh air filled my nostrils, filling me with comfort.

The walk home passed by quickly. There was no sense of dread like the time I had found Isaac dead in front of the shop. Setting my papers on the dining room table, I headed straight towards my bedroom to take a nap. Warren had said to take a break, and there was nothing better than escaping off to dreamland.

Sleep came easily as soon as I slipped between the sheets, the warmth instantly taking me off to dreams of magic, giving me glimpses of what I could have been had I stayed and learned how to wield it instead of running away from it. The magic swirled in the air as it danced around me, only for it to shatter away. My heart pounded against my chest as I shot up in bed. A feeling of dread settled in my stomach and I knew better than to ignore it. With hesitation, I slipped out of my bed to inspect my home. I had a feeling that I wasn't alone anymore. Something had happened to jerk me out of my slumber. Pressing an ear against my closed bedroom door, I waited with bated breath to hear footsteps on the other side. Only silence greeted me. I looked around my room, trying to see if anything could be used as a weapon.

Nothing.

In the living room, things waited to be unpacked. With all my energy spent at the shop, it left little motivation to do the same for my home. With no weapon in sight, I just had to hope luck was on my side as I slowly pulled open the door to step into the hallway. So far, no one showed up at the noise of the door opening, which was good. The dread in my stomach lowered as I made my way to the living room and dining room. Everything was the same in the living room; it was the dining room that had me pausing as I took in my dining room table. Before heading off to bed, I had placed my notes on the table to review after I woke up. That wouldn't be happening anymore. My notes were gone. Instead, there was a single piece of paper with a newsletter cut out letters, leaving me a message. A very clear warning.

Get out of town.

A warning I wouldn't be able to listen to because, just like I had told Isaac Cannon, I had nowhere else to go. Snowton Heights was my new home for the foreseeable future. Picking up the piece of paper, I traced over the message. It wasn't like I had unearthed a lot of information, but maybe I had figured out something important. And now someone other than Isaac Cannon wanted me out of town.

Maybe moving here was a bad idea after all?

My gaze drifted towards the front door, where there was a hole in the glass. A brick lay on the ground, and my front door was unlocked. That was how they got in, and the feeling of unease doubled as I stared at the broken glass. Shivers coursed up my body at the thought of someone in my home while I slept.

Coming here was a bad idea.

Chapter 18

The Wayward Shop of Mysteries was closed for business. Partly due to the fact I had no products, but also because there were more pressing things to figure out. There was the Wayward curse, the death of Isaac Cannon, and then there was the get out-of-town note. I could not forget that.

"I heard about what happened. Are you okay?" Warren asked as I entered Sweet Tokens of Sugar. At this rate, this place was going to become my home. Something I wouldn't mind since it had to be safer than my own home.

"News sure does travel fast when a Wayward is involved," I muttered as I made my way over to the counter, setting my elbows on it and dropping my head into my hands, the weight of everything going on in the world bearing down on me.

"We may be a decent sized town, but we act more like a small community."

That was something he didn't have to remind me of. I had experienced it firsthand. Isaac Cannon had showed up out of the blue, followed by Officer Erickson, and the mysterious man. I couldn't forget the ladies who gossiped outside the shop. Everyone knew everything about everyone. The only thing was they weren't sharing it with we me or I would have figured out how all of this was connected.

"Whoever broke into my home took my notes."

"That's odd..." Warren muttered. "It wasn't like you had a lot to go off of."

"Exactly!" I whined as I clenched my fists in my hair in frustration. "At least they took my notes towards the start of my investigation and not at the end."

"Does that mean you are going to continue to look into it?" There was worry in Warren's tone. I couldn't blame him. I was half crazy to keep looking into this after someone breaking into my home, but this was my only course in life. There was no plan B, C, D, or any letter of the alphabet. This was all I had, and I needed to make it work.

"I have to. I have no choice." I slumped against the counter, pressing my cheek to the icy surface. "Not sure I could sleep well at night knowing whoever did that is still out there."

"Sounds like you are in need of a pick-me-upper!" Warren let loose a chuckle before placing a plate on the counter, trying to tempt me with another round of macaroons.

"Maybe another time." No matter how tempting they looked, I couldn't get distracted. And my stomach would thank me. I was spending a lot of time here, which meant eating more sweets than I had in a long time. "Maybe you can help me with something else?"

"Sure, anything for you." Warren rubbed at the back of his neck as he waited for my request.

"By chance, do you know where Isaac Cannon used to live?"

"I do believe at some point I did a delivery for him." Warren shifted towards the little computer he used for processing orders and leafed through his records to try to locate an address. While he worked, I took the chance to examine the contents in the display box that were for sale today. While I wasn't in a mood to consume more sweets, it didn't mean I couldn't admire them. Warren was wonderful at his job, after all. And if everything went well today, then maybe, just maybe, I could reward myself with a small treat.

"Ah-ha! I found it!" Warren exclaimed before I could mentally consume the sweets that I couldn't eat. He turned the screen in my direction, pointing at the address right under Mr. Isaac Cannon. "I assume we are going to his place to investigate?"

"We?" I questioned.

"Of course," Warren answered quickly as he stepped out from behind the counter. "No way I'm letting you go alone."

"Thanks."

"Plus, this is a kind of fun."

I couldn't help but laugh. I was glad someone was having fun, because I sure was not. Being threatened by Isaac, coming across his dead body, meeting mysterious people, and having a brick thrown in my window was the furthest thing from fun in my mind. But I would welcome Warren's company. It would ease my worry as I ventured further into the unknown, trying to put the pieces together.

"Are we walking, or do you have a car?" I asked as we made our way out of Sweet Tokens of Sugar. There was no need to have a car in New York City as it was more of a hassle to have one than to go without. Here in Snowton Heights? It wouldn't be a bad idea; it would come in handy. Especially right about now.

"I may not have a car but ... I have a bike," Warren said, his hand going to rub at the back of his neck as he turned the corner to walk down the small alley between his shop and his neighbor's.

"A bike is for one person unless you have two."

"Well, it has two seats." Warren let loose a nervous chuckle as he pointed to the bike leaning against the back wall of the bakery.

"You have a tandem bike?" My eyebrows furrowed together as I took in the bike.

"April likes it. Great for bonding time, and it's excellent exercise."

I watched Warren pick the bike off the wall and wheel it away. While it wasn't as fast as a car, it would function a lot better than walking.

"You want to ride front or back?"

A laugh escaped at the awkwardness on Warren's face, as he couldn't look me in the eye. I was hoping I wasn't mirroring his discomfort, because the longer we stood here the weirder things would become. Riding a tandem bike was an odd thing to do, but it wasn't the oddest thing. Just extremely uncommon.

"You can ride front since you know where to go."

Warren gripped the tandem bike and pulled it out from the alley as I followed after him. After a few awkward stumbles as we tried to get in sync, Sweet Tokens of Sugar and Wayward Shop of Mysteries faded out of sight as we rode down the strip. Part of my focus was on the road ahead, of what I could see from sitting behind Warren, and the other half was focused on making sure I was in sync with the man. The last thing we needed was another tumble to the ground.

"You doing okay back there?" my riding partner called as we biked past the park. It was a nice day as the wind brushed against us. If I didn't have a million things to take care of, it would have been a perfect day to grab a book, a cup of hot tea and some sweets, and lie out in bask in the sun.

"Yeah, I'm fine!" I answered.

"We are almost there, just a bit longer."

I nodded my head even though he couldn't see me. Warren kept his gaze fixated straight ahead, leading us to our destination to gather more clues.

Chapter 19

I wasn't sure what to expect when walking through the home of the person who died in front of my shop. But it wasn't what was in front of me. With the tandem bike parked outside, and some laughs exchanged between the neighbors and Warren, who seemed to have a good reputation with everyone in town, we were pointed in the direction of where to find the spare key to the home.

Upon entry into the second-story apartment, there was a table to the side that held a bowl overfilled with junk. Mail scattered around the bowl, some open and some left untouched. After quickly leafing through them, they were all addressed to Isaac Cannon, so he lived alone.

"What exactly are we looking for? I haven't done this before," Warren said as he riffled through the letters right after me.

"Neither have I," I answered as I continued into the home. Hopefully, he didn't mind that we were searching his place. Though I doubt he could say much from where he was. The little entryway opened onto an area that split between being a living room and a kitchen. The kitchen was a mess, overrun by takeout boxes on the counter. And as I stepped further into the room, the smell that I hadn't noticed before became apparent. My nose twitched as I inhaled the fumes that had to be nearing toxic levels. Inching closer to the kitchen, I confirmed the scent was coming from there. There must be left over food in the boxes, trash not taken out or something, because this bad smell was not natural.

I plugged my nose as I turned towards the living room and I called back to Warren. "You take the kitchen and I'll take the living room." There was no way I was going to be searching that kitchen.

"Why do I get the kitchen?" Warren asked as he stepped forward, his own fingers flying up to pinch his nose.

"You are more familiar with the kitchen than I," I answered before making my grand escape. In the living room, I could hear the grumble that Warren let loose, but he made his way over to the kitchen anyway. He was the one who'd wanted to tag along, and for that I was grateful.

I focused my attention on the area tasked to me, taking stock of what I would need to search. The couch was pulled out into a makeshift bed, sheets and pillows thrown out lazily on the pull-out mattress. Isaac Cannon was not one to make his bed. Carefully picking up a pillow, followed by a sheet, I inspected the bed to see if anything was tucked under the messy sheets. Nothing. Changing course, I leaned over, pulling up the mattress to look underneath to see if the age-old hiding spot was in use, but again came up short.

"How is it going over there?" Warren called over to me, his voice slightly high-pitched. Dropping the mattress, I looked over to the kitchen where Warren stood, one hand rummaging around while the other pinched his nose.

"Nothing so far," I answered as I watched him pick up a dirty cloth before dropping it.

Nothing seemed off with the pullout bed, so I shifted my attention over to the end tables, instantly zeroing in on a facedown picture frame. Curiosity got the best of me. I flipped it over.

Isaac Cannon stood in front of a garden, his arm wrapped around the shoulders of a female, one who looked familiar. She had a smile on her face but Isaac didn't. There was a scowl. I sat on the bed, a creak emitting from the weight. Where did I know her from? I needed to figure out who she was, because she was someone important. Big enough in Isaac's life that her picture was on his end table, even if it was facedown. The bed creaked again as a weight joined me.

"Found something?" Warren inquired as he looked at the picture in my hand. "I didn't know Isaac and Sara were close."

"Sara?" I muttered as I examined the female again.

"Sara Alma, didn't you meet her?"

There was no way this was the same person from the nightclub. But the longer I stared, and a bit of squinting of the eyes, the more she started to resemble the person I had met. Just minus all the heavy makeup.

"Do you think they were dating?" I asked as I took stock of how close they were standing. Isaac had his arm around her shoulders; their bodies were pressed together as she leaned into his side. And as I put the picture frame closer to my face, I could make out some fingers on the opposite side of Isaac that were heavily obstructed by his baggy sweater. They had wrapped their arms around each other.

"If not, then at least close friends."

"This means Isaac and Sara knew each other," I said as I placed the frame on my lap. "Does this mean he also has a personal connection with the others?"

"According to the takeout in the kitchen, I would say yes."

"What does takeout have to do with that?" I asked, puzzled. I turned to face him, stealing a quick glance in the kitchen at the takeout boxes.

"Well, it's from the same place Adam Dunlap takes cooking classes from. A restaurant runs the school," Warren answered, his hand coming to rub at the back of his neck.

My mouth dropped as the cogs in my head spun wildly, till it clicked. Quickly, I stood as I looked over at the kitchen. I wasn't eager to actually go over into the kitchen.

"Others take class there as well?"

Warren nodded as I continued to stare at the takeout boxes. It didn't mean Isaac and Adam knew each other. But it also could mean they did, in fact, know each other. With the amount of containers on the counter, I was thinking it likely they'd had a run-in at some point.

"It looks like you are connecting the dots."

I placed a hand on Warren's shoulder as I pursed my lips, my mind still trying to figure out the possible paths. "I'm trying to," I muttered. "Isaac Cannon knew Sara Alma, and there is a very good chance he knew Adam Dunlap as well..." I trailed off as I finally tore my gaze away from the kitchen to look around the small apartment. "What about the mysterious man? Did Isaac know him too?" I turned to look at the end table to see if there was anything else on there that would indicate Isaac knew that last person. But how was I going to tie them together when I knew nothing of the man?

"We need to keep searching. There has to be something here..." I muttered as I left Warren to search anything I managed to get my hands on. There was a bathroom off to the side, but first I pivoted to the entertainment stand in the living room. Best to sweep every room before moving on to the next. My fingers glided against the top shelf of the cabinet and a thin layer of dust attached to my finger. A small shiver rocked through my body—dust and I weren't friends. Moving on to the second shelf, the bigger of the two, there were several books that drew my attention. Gliding my fingers across the spines of the books, I paused on the biggest one. *A History of Hats.* There was a little piece of string sticking out of it, so I removed the book to see where he had left off. The first thing I saw was the word "mercury" next to the chapter Isaac had left off on. As I cracked it open more to read, something fluttered to the ground. Making sure to not lose my place in the book,

I bent down and picked up the piece of paper, my hands shaking.

It resembled the note that was left at my house.

"Warren!" I yelled as I turned towards him as I held up the paper up to him.

"Does that say what I think it says?"

I nodded in my head in response, the paper tightly gripped between my fingers. The person who did this note used the same method of cutting out letters from magazines. And there was only one person we were still trying to find a connection with and there was only one person who didn't want us looking into their family.

I paid your price. Stop looking into my family and the Wayward curse or ELSE!

Chapter 20

I sat on the stool, staring at the cauldron in the middle of the back room. The rust was still evident on the pot despite trying my best to remove it. It wouldn't come off easily; it would take a lot more elbow grease.

"Should I buy a new one?" I muttered as I pursed my lips. It was an item that had history, not one I could easily replace. And it wasn't like I could just order a giant cauldron and have it delivered with no one raising their eyebrows. With a deep sigh, I slouched forward, crossing my arms over my chest. The pot would stay.

There was no doubt about it, I was trying to occupy my mind with something else so I didn't have to think about the more pressing matters. Like the fact that everyone impacted by the Wayward curse knew each other. A connection all with Isaac, who was dead. It was obvious the letter in the house was from the mysterious man. And Isaac had bitten off more than he could chew. Did he attempt to blackmail the mysterious man, and that was why the note said he had paid his price? But there was the "or else" part. Could that mean he was there to kill Isaac?

"Arghh!!" I screamed in frustration as I made fists in my hair. This was supposed to be a clean slate, a new start to rediscovering the magic of my childhood. And instead I was getting twisted in a web that I couldn't find my way out of. How was everything I managed to find out so far supposed to make sense? What the heck was going on in this town? Frustration got the best of me as I kicked out at the cauldron pot, pain shooting through my toes as I hopped on one foot, gripping my throbbing foot as I tried to rub out the pain. When I felt the throb die down, I promptly made my way out of the back room. I needed something to take my mind off things or who knew what I would do next.

"There you are…"

I froze, the door to the back room clicking shut as I moved into the front part of the shop. I stared into the brown eyes of the man who'd caused so many questions and left no answers.

"Hello..." My words came out slowly as I observed the man. He wasn't wearing all white like last time. This time he was wearing black slacks, with a black button-down shirt that still had several buttons undone, exposing his chest, where his gold chain was on display.

"You made great progress in your research." He walked forward, slow steps. The air felt heavier with every one he took. Thankfully, he stopped when he reached the counter, returning to the position he had taken before, where he sat at the edge, one leg propped up.

"Thanks," I muttered, unsure of how I was supposed to answer him.

"Great progress despite being here such a short time..." he drawled out, clasping his hands together as he motioned to the chair at the counter, beckoning me to come closer to him. I didn't fall for it. There was something odd about this man and, as of right now, I barely knew anything about him. That was one reason not to trust him. But I knew in my gut he knew more about Isaac's death than he was willing to let on, and that was enough to keep me rooted in place.

"Come." He tapped the counter, his lips curving slightly upward. "Just thought I would offer some more information."

Information?

Could it be possible?

"That is what you want, right?"

It was. But did I dare accept the information from the man? With a heavy sigh, I stepped forward until I was able to take a seat at the counter. Looking right up into his eyes, his lips curved into the biggest grin I had ever seen.

"What information do you have?" I asked. I felt like a little kid, baited with candy.

"I know you found that a relationship exists between Isaac Cannon and Sara Alma."

My mouth dropped. How did he know that? In order for him to know I had made the connection between Sara and Isaac, he had to know I had been Mr. Cannon's apartment. But if he knew that, he was following me, keeping tabs on my activity.

Mustering courage, I uttered the question that was on repeat in my mind: "Who are you?"

"Just someone who doesn't want things to come to light."

Like murder?

"Like what?" I pressed, replacing the word *murder* so I didn't come right out and accuse him.

"That," he whispered, leaning in closer till his breath was hot against my cheek, grin still etched on his face, "is for you to never find out." He reached out and tucked a piece of hair behind my ear before hopping off the counter.

"Why are you here?" I whispered.

"To give you information."

I bit my tongue. This was the most we had ever spoken, and all I had gotten were more questions. Who was he? And was he dangerous?

He pulled back his shoulders, stuffing one hand in his pocket and the other trailing up and down the counter as he stared at me. It set me on edge the longer we watched each other.

"I'll give you a little information to look into Isaac's death..." he said, his fingers still trailing across my counter. He held his hand up as if he wanted a handshake. "But you can't look into the curse. Do we have a deal?"

I stared out at his outreached hand. Was he implying that they weren't connected? That Isaac Cannon's death was not somehow linked to the Wayward curse? He hadn't been here when I had my encounter with the now dead man. Or maybe he was? I narrowed my eyes as there was a chance he was watching me before he had walked into my shop the day we met.

"I don't understand..."

He frowned, his hand lowering slightly. "Do we have a deal or not?"

There were only a few options I had to pick from. I could ignore his deal and continue to look into both, but he wouldn't go away. He didn't peg me as the type of guy that took no for an answer. If I turned him down, I would have to sleep with both eyes open and constantly look over my shoulder. Or I could agree to his deal. Look into Isaac Cannon's death but not the Wayward curse. But if they somehow ended up being linked like I thought, then what? I could kill two birds with one stone. While still not walking on eggshells.

"Yes."

I just hoped I didn't come to regret agreeing to his deal when I didn't even know his name.

"Good." He leaned in close as he whispered in my ear. "Mr. Cannon and Ms. Alma had been dating for a long time until recently." He shifted a little closer, the hairs on the back of my neck standing on edge, but I stayed still, not pulling away even if the urge was strong. "It ended in a big fight, causing a huge scene." The mysterious man pulled back and gave me a nod before turning on his heels and heading towards the front of the shop to leave.

"Wait!" I shouted, standing up from my chair. "That's it? That is the information you had to share?"

He did a dismissive wave, "Of course!" he called back as the bell above the door jingled. "I'm sure you and Warren can put two and two together."

I watched the man leave the shop, too stunned to follow after him. In part, due to the important information he had to share was just confirming that Isaac and Sara had been dating, and there was some huge scene due to them breaking up. The other part of why I didn't want to follow after him was because he had mentioned Warren by name. The mysterious man was indeed watching me. The mere thought of it made my skin crawl as I rushed outside. The mysterious man was already long gone. Despite knowing that just because I couldn't see him didn't mean he wasn't around, I rushed across the street to Sweet Tokens of Sugar.

"Serafina, back already?" Warren asked as he waved in greeting. He wasn't alone though, for leaning against the counter was Adam Dunlap. There had to be something in the air to not only bring the mysterious man to my shop, but Adam Dunlap to Warren's bakery.

"I just wanted to tell you something I found out," I started as I stepped forward.

Adam turned to face me, his eyebrow raised slightly. "What did you find out?"

I bit my lip, debating on answering him. He had provided some information the last time we spoke, nowhere near as mysterious as the man who I didn't have a name for. But could I trust what he would say? I guess there was only one way to find out.

"By chance, did you deliver food to Isaac Cannon?"

"Pretty often. He was always willing to try some dishes I was working on." He turned back to Warren, exposing a bag on the counter as he patted at it. "Just like I just dropped something off for Warren." He lifted the bag off the counter and shook it, a smile on his face. The logo on the bag matched the bags that were in Isaac Cannon's apartment. One of the first answers of the day: Adam Dunlap had known Isaac Cannon and had visited his place. Now would I be able to glean more information from him?

"Did you deliver food to him the day he died?"

"I did." Adam cocked his head to the side as he answered, his eyes going wide as he looked to Warren and then back at me. He pointed to himself as he spoke. "Wait! You don't think I had anything to do with his death, do you?"

"I didn't say that," I quickly responded. I was just here trying to make the connection between everything, but if Adam wanted to explain how everything worked together, then I would let him.

"I had nothing to do with his death. He was a good guy most of the time, except for his mood swings. I swear! He was just someone needing a bit of help."

I pursed my lips. "What about Sara Alma?"

"His ex-girlfriend?" Adam responded as he cupped his chin and looked off into the distance. "The last I heard, they called it quits and went their separate ways."

So the mysterious man had provided valid information after all when he had said Sara and Isaac had dated at one point and had broken up. It was hard to trust information from an untrustworthy source, but having Adam confirmed it helped.

Unless they were working together.

I wanted to groan in frustration at the change of thought. With the mysterious man watching me, I had to be more careful.

"Thank you for the information, Adam."

"I can't have you thinking I had anything to do with it." He smiled. "I don't think Sara had anything to do with it as well."

"Why you say that?" This time it was Warren who spoke up, drawing Adam's attention to himself.

"Their breakup was a mutual thing, no bad feelings."

I stared at Adam in bewilderment. The mysterious man had said there was a big scene from their breakup, but now

Adam was saying something different. Someone had to be lying ... but who?

#

Chapter 21

Warren leaned on the counter as he played with the supplies still there. We had locked the door to his bakery, and made our way to the back in the kitchen to be out of sight once Adam had walked out. It was the only way to make sure we weren't being spied on.

"Someone has to be lying," I started as I paced in the kitchen, my hand cupping my chin. I had told him everything that happened with the mysterious man and how his tidbit of information clashed with Adam's. "Let's go back to the beginning."

"To the start of the Wayward curse? I don't know that much history about it," Warren stated as he stopped fiddling with his baking supplies and rubbed at the back of his neck.

I couldn't help but smile. Despite the knowledge that we were being watched, he still somehow managed to lighten the mood. Warren was a great source of knowledge, but this time we didn't need to go that far back in history to figure out what was going on. Because I finally understood what the mysterious man was getting on about when he had me agree to look into the Wayward curse. They were connected, but in the end, they were two separate incidents.

"Let's start with the day he died."

"That might be a good start," Warren answered as I leaned on the counter opposite of him, our heads almost touching as we tried to combine brainpower to figure out what had happened the night everything changed.

"You left the shop and hadn't seen Isaac Cannon that day, correct?" Warren questioned.

"Right."

"And then you turned back?"

"I did," I replied.

"Why did you turn back? Did you happen to see something?"

Did I happen to see something? *No*. Did I happen to feel something? *Yes*. I chewed on my bottom lip as I thought of a reply. A sixth sense had occurred, and because of that, I had decided to go back the way I came, ultimately stumbling upon the dead body of Isaac Cannon. But I knew it wasn't just a simple sixth sense, it was latent magic, but exposing that would only complicate things. And with everything going on, I didn't want to complicate things even more. So I settled on responding with a simple explanation. "It was just a bad feeling."

"A bad feeling that ended up with you finding a dead body." Warren tapped at his chin. "Were you still near the shop at least, or almost home?"

I replayed the events of the dreadful night in my head. After closing up shop, I had stopped by the bakery and then headed home. It was only after passing the park and getting to that streetlamp when the feeling of dread kicked in. In the end, I hadn't made it that far away from the shop. My mouth dropped as I snapped my fingers at the realization.

"I was still close by, so whoever did it had to be near as well," I exclaimed. "So where was everyone the night he died?"

"Well, Adam said he was at class. Sara was working the charity event, and the mysterious man was a guest at the event," Warren answered, laying out the clues that we had gathered. Clues that we had to hold on to mentally because my notes had been stolen. We had three people to look into, three families.

"The mysterious man is the most … mysterious," I started, unable to think of another word to describe the man that provided just enough information that it could be classified as information but enough to really provide leads. "He is withholding a lot of information." I rested my elbow on the counter as I leaned my head in my hand as the image of the man who wore white one day and black another day popped into my head. "We really needed to figure out who he is." That would be impossible. He only popped up when he wanted to pop up. Next time I ran into him, though, I would have a slew of questions so our time together wouldn't be wasted.

"Should we question Adam again?"

"Tonight?" I inquired.

"He is in class tonight if you are free," Warren replied. I shrugged and nodded; it wasn't like I had other things to do in Snowton Heights. Warren smiled and picked up his cell phone, asking the person on the other end to feed April dinner, telling them he would be home later than normal. Before hanging up, he covered the phone and whispered, "My brother," before talking to April and letting her know what was going on. I hadn't asked who he was on the phone with, but smiled anyway. "All set."

We made our way down the street. There was a bite to the air today. I rubbed at my arms covered in a sweater. Stuffing my hands into the pocket of my pants to help take the chill off my hands, we settled in synchronized step. We walked in silence as we passed by shops, the majority of them already closed down for the night.

The walk was comfortable as we came upon the park. A couple sitting on the bench drew my attention before shifting to someone running down the trail. With everything going on trying to re-open the Wayward Shop of Mysterious, solve Isaac Cannon's death while somehow looking into but not looking into the Wayward curse, I hadn't had a chance to really stop and enjoy my new town. Snowton Heights was the complete opposite of New York City. Businesses there stayed open well into the night, and if things weren't open it felt like everything was, by how busy the streets stayed and the constant lights. There were a million things to do in the city to the point it was overwhelming, and I did nothing—working all day and the transit to and from work would drain my time, leaving very little to enjoy. But it was all different here. I took a big breath of air as we finally passed the park and continued on our walk.

"You're quiet. Everything okay?"

"Just thinking about life before moving out here."

"I bet it was a lot simpler." Warren did an awkward smile as he rubbed the back of his neck. "Didn't have a Wayward curse to worry about."

"That may be true, but maybe it's what I needed," I replied.

"The drama?" Warren let loose a chuckle.

"That is just a bonus."

Our walk continued in silence until we reached the cooking school that Adam took his classes at. Peering through the glass windows, we could see several classes were in progress. Students in their white chef coats sat two to a table while a teacher stood in the front, working on a meal. It was hard to see what the teacher was cooking, other than it contained lots of fruit and would be very sweet. Before I could examine more of the class, there was a knocking sound as Warren tapped on the window.

Heads turned in our direction and Adam stood, staring at us. Warren was the last person I would have thought would knock on a window to grab someone's attention as they sat in a class filled with peers. Adam stood up, walking right past his teacher, who was shooting us a dirty look, and made his way out of the classroom to come outside.

"Good job," I whispered harshly to Warren as I shoved my elbow into his side for drawing so much attention. If looks could kill, then the teacher would have murdered us by now, and that would be horrible, for we already had one dead body on our hands.

"She's doing it wrong anyway. Might as well interrupt her class."

"What is she making?"

"A fruit tart. How she is able to mess that up is beyond me."

Considering I didn't know how to know make a fruit tart in the first place, I just nodded in agreement while mentally making a note to not make sweet things in front of Warren.

"What are you guys doing here?" Adam asked as he jogged over to where we stood. He did a slight wave to his teacher as she stuck her nose back in the air, barked something out to the class, and everyone went back to watching her make the fruit tart incorrectly.

"We had some additional questions. Figured it would be best to ask them right away."

Adam rested his hands on his hips, raising his eyebrow. "Alright, then."

"Do you know of a man who wears a white suit or black suit, a few buttons undone with a gold chain?" I blurted.

"I can't say I do. Most of my time is occupied with working or classes. It doesn't leave much time to interact with people who can afford to wear gold chains," he replied, his lips curving down into a frown. "This got to deal with Isaac Cannon's death?"

I nodded. "The mysterious man was also impacted by the Wayward curse and knew Isaac."

"Can't say I know who you are talking about, but honestly I had nothing to do with Isaac's death. He was nice if not a little crazy, but it wasn't me. Yeah, everyone called it a curse and my family lost their business because of it, but it was a blessing in disguise. Just took a few years for us to realize that."

"A blessing? What do you mean?" I inquired, confused. From the way Isaac had approached me, there was nothing *blessing* about the Wayward curse.

Adam placed a hand on his heart. "I'm Scottish and my family had a restaurant selling traditional meals you wouldn't find just anywhere." He pulled at his white coat as he fidgeted slightly. "We had one dish that was a bit risky, our best seller, which had some legal crackdown after we closed. Which saved us from being caught up in it."

"You were making something with illegal ingredients?"

"Well, not illegal ingredients," he started as he tossed a look into the classroom before focusing back on me. "Americans just have a different view on things. Like making dishes with horses is common in some places in the world but not here."

I pulled back from Adam, perplexed and disturbed by horse food. "Your family," I mumbled, "made dishes with horses?" My words were drawn out as I processed that his family actually sold meals with horses with it. Horses were magnificent animals, and while I didn't grow up riding them, I couldn't imagine biting into one at dinner while we talked about the day.

"Not horses, it was just an example!" Adam exclaimed as he waved his hands about. "It was actually sheep lung. Haggis tastes amazing, but it was the wrong time for my family to be selling haggis."

Haggis.

I hadn't eaten haggis, but I had heard about it. It had been frowned upon years ago because sheep lung at the time wasn't allowed to be imported. The Dunlaps considered it a blessing since they had shut down before haggis blew up in the media. I pursed my lips, wondering if my grandparents knew that was going to happen and did something about it.

"I really need to get back to class. Missing out on making a great dessert. But honestly, I had nothing to do with Isaac's death. I swear it." For added measure, he raised his hand as if he were doing a Scout's promise."

Without waiting to see if we had any further questions, Adam waved goodbye and jogged back into the building.

A moment later, he reappeared in the classroom, receiving a dirty look from the teacher as he made his way back to his seat.

"That was extremely helpful," Warren said beside me. He had been quiet through my conversation with Adam. I had almost forgotten he was beside me.

"You know?" I started as I turned on my heels to walk back to my shop, "I think I actually might believe him. That he had nothing to do with it." My gut had filled with dread the night Isaac Cannon had died. But around Adam? It was still. Adam was like a book. Once cracked open, he spills everything. He just seemed like an overly nice person.

The mysterious guy, on the other hand ... a closed book that held on to its secrets.

Chapter 22

Rain poured outside as I stared out the window watching people walk by on the street. With nothing to sell yet, there was no reason to call people to come in and browse my wares. But soon I would have something. I stared down at the notebook in front of me that listed several products that would serve nicely as my very first products for my grand opening. *Food* was scratched out. While the need for food was universal, I just wasn't equipped to cook like Warren. Instead, I stared at the item I had circled: *beauty*. From there it broke off into an additional list that included face masks, moisturizers, and hair products. Beauty was a safe area to get into because everyone wanted something and it functioned as great gifts as well. Now the only thing was to narrow down which item I should focus on first.

The bell above my door jingled as I looked up to see who had entered the empty Wayward Shop of Mysteries.

"How are things going over here?" Warren asked as he stepped in, shaking off some of the rain that had gathered on him from his short walk over. Setting down my pen, closing the notebook, I tucked it all away. No reason for him to see I had magical face masks and other magical terms written.

"Just brainstorming."

"Need any help?" Warren asked as he made his way over to my counter to stand on my side, his gaze shifting to my closed notebook I had just tucked away.

"Not yet. Was trying to think about something other than death and curses."

Warren rubbed at the back of his neck. "Well, that's why I came over. I got to thinking," he started as he placed his hands on the counter. "I agree. I don't think Adam had a play in Isaac's death." With his left hand, he reached out in front of me, using his index finger to point to a random spot on the counter.

"What are you doing?" I inquired as I watched him place his right hand on the desk on as well, using two fingers to point at the exact same spot before leaning over and using his thumb to place it close to the counter's edge. At a glance, it looked like a triangle.

"Pretend it's a map. Adam was here." Warren wiggled his finger on his left hand before continuing: "And Sara and the mysterious man were here." Warren then wiggled the two fingers grouped together on the right side. "These two were closer together." His right hand wiggled, showing the nightclub where the charity was held and my shop. "Adam was in the direction you were walking, so there would have been a good chance you would have passed him at some point."

I rested my elbow on the counter as I analyzed his finger map. Warren did have a point. The location of the cooking class was significantly farther away from the Wayward Shop of Mysterious than the nightclub. If Adam had been at class all night like he had said, he would have to been one super-fast man to make it out of class, pass me to kill Isaac, and run past me again to get back to class. And the way his teacher got irritated when we had pulled him out just for a few minutes made me really doubt he could have done it without being seen. Which meant it had to be one of the people at the charity ball, but who?

I cocked my head to the side as I placed my hand next to his right hand and did a mini walk with my index and thumb to where he had positioned my shop. It took a few steps due to the difference in hand size.

"Sara Alma and the mysterious man were both at the charity ball that night. With the amount of people that had to be at the charity, they would have easily been able to sneak out and back in without really causing a scene." I moved my hand back to the finger that indicated the club as I held it there against Warren's hand. "They would have been able to go in and out of the club without ever running into me..." I trailed off as I turned to Warren and clicked my fingers. "One of them is the culprit!"

Warren nodded eagerly as he finally broke his finger map to adopt a thinking pose. I mimicked him as I thought about the two people we needed to question.

"How do we question them if we don't know the identity of one?" I asked. That was the biggest problem and the longest unanswered question. With one suspect in the wind, and no way to track him down, we would have to find a way to lure him back out. "Let's go back to Isaac Cannon's house."

"Why?"

"Maybe there is something we missed and we need to draw out the mysterious man."

"When?" Warren asked as I looked around my empty shop.

"No better time than the present," I answered as I smiled and made my way towards the front of the shop, giving the empty shelves a glance. I couldn't wait till all of this was sorted and I could open up for business.

"You think anything would have changed since we had last been there?" Warren asked after we'd made our way across the street to grab his tandem bike. Did I want something with Isaac Cannon's apartment to change since the last time we had been there? Yes, and no. Maybe someone left another clue or someone could have come and cleaned out his place. Regardless of what might happen, we were about to find out.

Chapter 23

With the tandem bike resting against the grass, Warren grabbed the spare key from the place we had last retrieved it and we entered the apartment for the second time. Instantly overcome with a horrible smell, I plugged my nose. It was the exact opposite of entering Warren's bakery, where I would be instantly greeted with a sweetness that was often a mix of vanilla and cinnamon. Isaac's apartment reeked like a dead body. I glanced in the direction where I knew the source of the smell was coming from. The amount of bugs swarming around in the kitchen had tripled since last time. There was no way I was stepping into that area.

"I think you are on kitchen duty again," I muttered as my voice came out funny with my nose still plugged.

"I think a different set of eyes would be better, which means..." Warren touched the middle of my back before giving me a light push in the direction of the kitchen. "You should check it out."

"I think not," I quickly responded as I dove away from the kitchen, hurling myself into the living room that also functioned as a bedroom, the couch breaking my fall as it was still pulled out in a bed.

"I'm perfectly fine with searching over here."

With the hand not plugging my nose, I waved at Warren before pointing to the kitchen. It was already bad enough the smell had gotten worse since the last time we were here, but there was absolutely no way I was searching the kitchen. Not even the fact I was looking into Isaac's death could get me to go over there. Before Warren could protest and insist we switch spots, I pulled the sheets off the bed to see if anything lingered in between the layers. All that greeted me was emptiness.

"So many bugs..." Warren grumbled from the kitchen as I heard items shifting about. I did my best to not look in his direction, where he could potentially guilt trip me in switching. I went back to the end table. The picture frame was still there that exposed his relationship with Sara

Alma. But nothing else had changed to provide any new clues, so I walked over to the entertainment cabinet to look through it once more. Withdrawing the book from before, I opened to where the bookmark and letter was, only there was nothing. Shaking the book, nothing fell from between the pages.

"Warren…" I called to where my partner was still fumbling in the kitchen. He stopped making a racket and made his way to stand beside me.

"What is it?"

"It's not here," I responded.

"What's not here?" he asked as he reached for the book. I gladly let him have it as I fumbled with the rest of the items on the cabinet to see if we had accidentally misplaced it. "What am I looking for?"

"The note!" I exclaimed as I pointed to the book. "It's not here!" I motioned to the entertainment center. "It's gone!" It was gone like it never existed. "He had to have been here. But how would he know we would come back?"

"Mysterious man doing mysterious things sounds about right." Warren let loose a chuckle as he rubbed at the back of his neck.

"Maybe there is something here we are overlooking," I said as I turned around, taking in the small apartment once more. But what were we missing? "We need to keep searching."

"Not in the kitchen. I don't think anyone was messing around in there."

Warren probably had a point. Only a crazy person would venture into the kitchen to search it with that horrible smell and all those bugs. Plus, if Warren wasn't going to search it there was no way I was. So I continued to walk in a small circle, trying to eye everything of this small studio apartment that could be searched. The kitchen and living room/bedroom had been completed. But there was still the bathroom left and a closet.

"Can you check the bathroom?" I asked Warren as I pointed to the cracked-open door. With the letter being found the last time we were here, we had stopped investigating, leaving the bathroom unsearched till now. And while he searched that room, I made my way over to the closet. The one tucked right behind the front door. "I will be looking in the closet," I shouted so Warren would know where I was. He provided no reply. A tower of boxes greeted me with clothes tucked behind it as the closet was filled to the brim. There was no way I would be able to remove a box without sending the whole thing tumbling down on me. Good thing I'd brought muscle.

I smiled as I called out to Warren. "Can you lift this box for me?"

Warren made his way over, reached up, and removed the first box. He let loose a grunt as it took some wiggling to get it out before he set in the bed. The counter in the kitchen would have been more ideal, but it was already occupied with bugs. A moment of silence settled between us as we stared at the box. This was it. We were about to find out more information about Isaac Cannon. Taking in a deep breath, I removed the lid off the cardboard box to peer inside. The first thing that caught my eye were the picture frames. Picking up several, I held them up so Warren could peer at them as well. As he leaned in close, he pointed to the small boy in the picture. "That has to be Isaac."

The little boy in the picture did resemble the man who had died right in front of my shop.

"Then this must be his family. Sister..." I pointed to the little girl beside him who had the ends of her long blond hair curled, part put back and held in place by a large bow. She had an arm hooked around Isaac. Two adults stood behind them, both smiling wide and placing a hand on each of the kids' shoulders. "And these must be his parents. The ones impacted by the curse," I muttered. They looked like one big happy family, but disaster was about to strike them, and it was all because of a curse they blamed on my family.

Setting the picture aside, I reached into the box and withdrew another picture frame. They had aged in this one and, unlike the previous photo, they did not look as happy as before. The father being the most noticeable change. He looked like he'd aged a decade, but the minimal change in Isaac let me know a decade had not passed. His father had a top hat tucked into the crook of his arm, patches of his hair missing while the rest was smoothed out. That wasn't the most alarming thing though. He had blotches on his skin like a rash spreading. It appeared on the exposed skin of his hand that was resting on Isaac's shoulder, as well as on his neck that was exposed above the collar of his clothes.

"Do they look a little sick?" Warren whispered as he tapped the man I was just observing. It seems I wasn't the only one to notice the difference between the two. "Is this part of the curse?"

I mulled over Warren's question. For Adam Dunlap, the curse was a blessing in disguise. Bus Isaac had said it was a curse, and from the article it had impacted their business. But could it have also made them sick? No, that couldn't be possible.

"There has to be something else," I answered Warren.

I rifled around in the box, trying to find something else that could help identify what had happened to the Cannon family, but this box was just memories. Painful ones, I decided, as I glanced at the next photo. The degradation of the Cannon family was even more present as all family members grew sicker, as if they truly had been cursed.

"Should we try another box?" Warren asked. I nodded. He shifted away to walk over to the closet to remove another box while I set the photos back in the original box. It was too painful to continue to look through this one.

Shifting my attention to the new box at my side, I pulled back the flaps and instead of pictures there were hats. An abundance of them as they popped out now that they were free from their cage. Upon picking up the first hat, it was easy to see that it matched the style Isaac Cannon's father wore.

"Why keep all the hats?" I inquired out loud, not expecting Warren to have an answer as I fumbled through the rest of the box, which contained hats of all the same style.

"Didn't they make hats?"

It was true that they made hats, and that could be why he kept them all. But for some reason I felt like I was missing something. The Dunlaps' curse turned into a blessing because of the import issue. There had to be something more at play than just a hat factory shutting down. There had to be a reason for all of it, but I couldn't just put my finger on it.

\#

Chapter 24

My mind was abuzz as I made my way to the library once more. It held all the information of the world in one spot, and I was hoping it would provide some kind of clue on what I could be missing.

My fingers typed away, inputting a flurry of keywords in hopes of trying to narrow down the search to something that would tell me what else might be at play. No matter the string of keywords, nothing popped up. A random combination of *hat*, *balding*, *rash*, *curse* and a mix of other things that popped up in my mind resulted in nothing.

"Do you need any help?"

I turned towards the librarian, who had walked up to me while I sat using the computer. She must have gotten worried by my furious typing and sighs of defeat. I felt my cheeks heat up just thinking about how crazy I must have looked. But she didn't look bothered. She had a smile on her face, her blond hair pulled up into a neat bun, glasses on the bridge of her nose as she peered down at me. The very definition of friendly, but all librarians looked friendly unless one was making noise. Then that was a different story.

"Maybe?" I responded as I glanced at the computer before scratching at my chin and turning back to the librarian. "It's not really book related though."

"No problem. Let's see if I can help, anyway."

"I'm trying to make a connection between losing hair, rashes on the skin and, as weird as it sounds, hats."

"Loss of hair? Rashes? And hats?" she muttered as she pursed her lips and pushed her glasses up her nose. "Not present day, correct?"

"Correct. All of this would have happened years ago."

"Did they just wear hats or manufacture them?" she asked.

"Both."

"Ah!" She snapped her fingers as she gave me a big smile. "Have you looked into something called the mad hatter's disease?"

"Mad hatter's disease?" I questioned.

"Of course. It's not just in Wonderland that there is a mad hatter. It's a very real thing. Workers at hat factories were being infected by mercury that was being used in the production of hats."

I stared at the computer as I typed in mad hatter diseases. Articles upon articles populated on the screen. It was real! That was what was on the tip of my tongue. Mad hatter's disease. Clicking on the first link, it went into detail about the history of it, but it was too hard to find the symptoms. After clicking on a medical link that neatly outlined the symptoms, it listed rashes and hair loss as some physical symptoms. But the main thing about this disease was the internal symptoms that impacted the nervous system. I bit my bottom lip as I mulled over what I was reading. Could this also be why Isaac had been so hostile towards me? It would be impossible to know for sure until I figured out the true reason behind his death.

"Thank you very much!" I exclaimed as I gave the librarian a quick hug. "This has been helpful!"

"Glad to be of help. If you need anything else, just let me know." With those parting words, the librarian walked off, leaving me alone. It was a short encounter, but it had been very useful as I logged off the computer to head over to Warren's bakery. He would want to know what I had found.

Chapter 25

"Did you manage to find something useful?" Warren asked as he looked up, smiling in my direction as I entered Sweet Tokens of Sugar. I nodded in reply as he went back to helping the lady standing in front of the counter.

"The librarian at the library was helpful," I answered as I made my way over to the counter to stand beside the lady as she finished paying for her box of sweets. She turned towards me as I took the moment to examine her, her hazel eyes boring into me while she wore a neutral expression.

"Serafina Wayward?"

I couldn't help but tilt my head slightly and raise my eyebrows as she spoke my name. The news of a Wayward back in town had sure traveled fast, and was still spreading. And along with the mention of me, there would have been mention of the curse trailing right behind it.

"Nice to finally meet you," she uttered as she held out her hand, waiting for me to shake it. While I still didn't know who she was, I reached out and took her hand. With an iron grip, she shook my hand, my mouth dropping slightly by how tight she was squeezing my hand, a hidden strength in her slim frame hid very well. The lady wore a long white sundress that went mid-leg, along with white chunky heels, black sunglasses, and a white wide-brim hat. Honestly, she didn't look like she was from Snowton Heights. She smelled and looked like money.

"My husband isn't too pleased that you are looking into our family."

Husband?

What was she talking about? The only person I was looking into was Isaac Cannon, who was currently dead. If she somehow ended up being married to Mr. Cannon, I wasn't sure what I would do. Furrowing my brow and giving Warren a look, who looked just as confused as I, I responded to the lady: "By chance, are you married to Isaac Cannon?"

"No."

That was good news and bad news. But the question still begged: who was she talking about?

"Who is your husband?" I asked as I watched her lift a hand up to finger the gold chain around her neck. She gave it a twirl before switching over to stroking the piece against her neck. The odd thing was that the piece looked familiar. As I took a step back, I realized everything about her felt familiar. A completely white outfit with a gold chain reminded me of the man who invited himself to sit on my counter. But it couldn't be?

Of course it had to be, because there was no one else.

"Oh, you've met him. Yes, that is my husband. Very sweet man, unless angered."

Unless angered?

I turned towards Warren, who was watching our inter-action unfold with a confused expression.

"Did I anger him?" I asked hesitantly, wondering if I was about to see the man again and if he was going to be less than pleasant.

"If you keep digging into our history, then yes, you will anger him," she answered as she grabbed her bag of sweets and tucked her wallet into her purse before giving Warren a nod and me a side glance and making to leave the bakery, only to pause as she pulled open the door, the bell above the door jingling.

"I'll give you this one thing so you stop angering my husband. We did business in one thing, and when the Wayward curse came about we were advised to change course or it would be our downfall. Some listened ... some didn't."

With no other words to utter, the woman in the all-white outfit made her way outside, the door closing behind her. Quickly, I rounded on Warren to figure out if he knew who she was.

"Do you know her name?"

"Unfortunately not, she always pays cash."

The mysterious man had just turned into a mysterious couple, and if it was hard getting information from one, it was about to be impossible to get information from both. Both of them looked like they came from money, and those with money could get away with doing bad things, like killing. But I wasn't sure if they killed Isaac though.

"What do you think she meant?" Warren asked.

I thought about it. They were very intent on protecting their family, living in their own little bubble from the outside world. And if Isaac was looking into them, then they could have had a hand in his death. But to do so in a public place where people were going to discover the body? That was the abnormal part that made it hard to believe it was them. They would have been leading a police investigation straight to their front doorstep.

"They did business in one thing..." Whatever that one thing was, according to the article, it made them millions. "They changed course to something else." Which was whatever they were doing in the present. "So why don't they want us looking into them? It has to do something with their current or previous business." That was the only logical answer. Either a past business or a current business was doing something illegal. Just like the Dunlaps, they must have been warned they were going to be hit with some type of legal crackdown and switched course. So if that was the case, who did that leave?

I placed four fingers on the counter as I thought out loud: "Four families. Dunlap, mysterious couple, Cannon, and Alma." I wiggled a finger as I said each name. "Dunlap changed businesses." I put a finger down. "Mysterious couple changed businesses." Another finger down, leaving me with two fingers. "Two families didn't change course, Cannon and Alma."

"And Cannon is dead," Warren whispered as I slowly nodded and put down another finger, leaving me with just one.

Together we spoke the last name that was still standing. "Alma."

\#

Chapter 26

True to Seattle weather, the sky outside was dark and gloomy. Rain pounded down as people in their raincoats walked about like everything was normal. Just another great day, and to them it probably was. Me though, I was still getting used to it. With my elbow resting on the counter, I stared across the street. There was a line in the bakery that reached the door. Despite the gloomy mood, people were still in the mood for sugar. My shop, on the other hand, was empty of people and of products on the shelves. Soon I would have products that would draw people in, and one day I would be just as busy as Warren. There were just two things standing in my way: creating the products, and figuring out how Sara Alma played a role in Isaac's death.

With a deep sigh, I relaxed in my chair and reached for my notebook, flipping to the page that had my list of products on it. Eventually I would need to gather the ingredients to create my first spell, but I had to put together a list of the stuff I needed first. Closing the notebook once more, I picked myself off the chair and headed towards the back room. There was only one trusty source of where to go to get magical information and that was a grimoire. Not any old grimoire, but one of my grandmother's.

The sound of a bell jingling grabbed my attention before I could dive into one of the boxes. I popped my head out of the back room to see the front door slowly closing.

"Hello?" I called as I stepped out of the back room fully, making sure to close the door behind me as I looked around my shop, trying to identify who might have walked in. My body tensed as I spotted a cloaked figure dressed in all black standing between two shelves. My gut twisted into a knot as I stared at the figure dripping from the rain. A hood covered their face.

"Hi," I started, somehow managing to gather my voice. "I'm not open yet."

They didn't respond, they just stood there. But I knew they were looking at me just like how I was looking at them.

"Can I help you?" I asked as I took a step forward, a hesitant one, as I was unsure if I should even be making my way closer to the figure. "Are you okay?" I jumped as the shop lit up for a moment as a crackle erupted outside. It had exposed part of the face hidden under the hood before the glow died down.

"Sara?" I asked as I remembered all those layers of make-up. "Sara Alma?' I questioned again. The figure pulled down her drenched hood and smiled, answering my question.

"Hi, Serafina."

"Is there something I can help you with?"

She reached into her pocket, pulling out a stack of cards. She set them on the counter before unzipping her jacket.

"I would like to read you about your future."

"My future? Any particular reason for the timing?"

It wasn't the worst timing, but it was for sure not even close to being the best timing. The rain pouring down, the random crackle, just made everything feel eerie. To have my fortune read on such a day just felt like a bad omen.

"Come sit." Sara pointed to my chair on the opposite side of the counter before picking up her cards and shuffling them. "You know, my mom taught me everything there is to know about the cards, in preparation for me to take over the business."

I shuffled forward, sitting down in my chair as she talked. A part of me still felt like this was a bad idea, but also another part wanted to know about my future.

"You probably want to know if you are on the right path," she started as she continued to shuffle her deck. "Of life. Of this new business. Of Isaac's death." Sara set the deck down on the counter and split it in half, before pulling the first card and setting it on the counter. With a light tap on the card to draw my attention, she said, "The Fool but upright. Foolish, most will say. A new journey of starting over at zero. Unaware of the unknown while embarking on a new adventure. Yet you step closer to the cliff. Shall we see where this new adventure in life takes you?" Sara pulled another card from the deck.

"Wheel of Fortune upright..." Sara looked at me as I looked up at her, holding her gaze. "What goes around must come around. Be kind and you shall receive kindness. Be mean and you shall receive hate. What started long ago must come full circle." Finally, she placed the third card on the counter as we both glanced down to see what it was.

"The World but reversed. Closure. Everything bubbles down to seeking closure on a personal issue. Family issue.

There is something big at play, but you aren't taking all the steps to fulfill it. You are missing something."

I looked at the three cards spread on the counter. I didn't know much about the cards, only that my family used them. With neglecting magic growing up, I couldn't tell what if what Sara said was true or not. But I could tell there was weight to her words.

The Fool. I had been blind my whole life, thinking that I needed to be normal. That magic was the only reason I was unhappy and the sole reason why I couldn't fit in with the other kids. It was the opposite. Magic made me unique. It just took me an extremely long time to figure that out, and now here I was embarking on a new journey, unsure of what was to come. As Sara stated, I was standing on the edge, just one step away from failing again.

Wheel of Fortune. What comes around must come around again. I had ran away from the magic side of my life and it had caught up to me. I was finally returning to my roots.

The World. The last card drawn but the biggest one. Sara had mentioned closure, and I was seeking closure in my life. That I had chosen the right path by pursuing magic. That the Wayward curse wasn't real and on figuring out what happened to Isaac Cannon.

But I had a feeling the cards didn't just apply to me. I stared at Sara. The cards also applied to her. She had to start a new journey when her mom didn't change course. She had stepped closer to the edge of the cliff in order to figure out who she was and who she could be. What goes around must come around. Our family issues started with her parents and my grandparents and they had come back around. And finally there was closure, something we both needed on the thing that brought us together in the first place. The Wayward curse. Isaac Cannon's death.

"Sara..." I started as she reached behind her back, slowly pulling something out. It took me a moment to realize what was happening. Never in a million years did I think I would be staring down the barrel of a gun. My stomach twisted into knots and I felt sick. I had come here to start a new life, and it was about to end abruptly. I had been a fool, stepped too close to the cliff, and it had come around full circle to bite me.

"If you just stayed away, I could have been happy," Sara said as her hand holding the gun shook. "Isaac and I were making amends. Learning to move on together. But you..." she growled as she thrust the gun in my face. "Seeing a Wayward here triggered him." She gripped her head, the gun smacking against her temple as she wavered back and forth. "Wayward this. Wayward that!" The words spat out of her mouth like they had been laced with ven-om. "Your family always has to ruin things! Always! You ruined my family. You ruined Isaac's family, and here you are acting like you don't know." She stepped closer, her body smacking against the counter. "All you had to do was stay away."

I slowly stood from my seat as I held up my shaking hands. I had to do something to defuse the situation. There was already one person dead; there was no reason to add to it.

"Sara..." I started, licking my lips as I willed myself to speak more. "Calm down. Surely we can—"

"Don't tell me to calm down!" she hollered, focusing the gun back on me again, right between my eyes. "Isaac was sick. Mercury from all the stupid hats his family liked to make. And seeing you made him worse." She let loose a growl as her arm slackened, the gun still pointed at me. "You triggered something in him. He wouldn't stop going on and on about the curse." Then there was the money..."

"Money?" I repeated.

"Money to shut us up." She slammed her hands on the table as I held my breath to see if the gun was going to be accidentally discharged. "But we couldn't let the Way-wards win again. Why couldn't we have our cake and eat it too?" She patted at her chest, her lips curving into a frown.

"It was supposed to be simple. Keep the money and get rid of you."

I backed away slowly as Sara stepped around the counter to follow after me, my pulse racing as she was still focused on me.

"Sara, what happened to Isaac?"

"He couldn't decide."

"Decide on what?" I pressed as I continued to inch back.

"One moment he wanted you gone and the next he wanted to leave. But why should we *leave*?" The word came out strained as she shouted at me.

"You don't have to. We can all live in harmony here," I responded, hoping she could understand I had nothing to do with the curse and there wasn't going to be a second coming of it.

"But we can't!" Her voice shook as the gun swung in the air. I flinched from the sudden movement. She was getting louder, more erratic. The longer this went on, the more unsure I was of what the outcome would be.

"You are here." She focused the gun on me again, her eyes wide. "The Waywards have to go, and since you are the only Wayward here..." She trailed off, but I knew what she meant by the way her lips curved upward.

"I have to go," I mumbled as I finished her train of thought. The only issue was that I didn't want to go. I had just started a new life, was making some friends. Not a lot, but was making progress. Things were different here already and they could be different for Sara too if she accepted help. So, silencing the alarms in my head, I took a step forward, causing her to cock her head to the side as she watched me.

"Sara, we can work this out."

"There is nothing to work out. My family is gone. Isaac is gone. There is nothing to work out." She was angry, there was no doubt about it, but then her voice grew soft. "We can't turn back time."

I somehow forced myself to give Sara a small smile despite her still pointing a gun at me. "No, but we can move forward."

"How? How can I when I poisoned the love of my life?"

I froze. She was the reason Isaac had fallen over dead right in front of the shop. He must have been in one of his moods, where she wasn't sure what he would do next, and she made the choice for him. A bad choice that cost him his life.

"We can get you help." I'd started thinking I was getting to her, but those were the wrong words. Her eyes grew wide, her pupils blown as she swung her arm about, almost hitting me in the head.

"Help? HELP? You and your family are the exact opposite of help!" she hollered as I watch her continue to swing the gun about, her whole body shaking as she tried to control some of her rage but failing miserably. Sara paced back and forth as she tried to figure out what to do next. I didn't have time to wait around while she decided. I needed to act fast before she made the same decision she made for Isaac for me. When she turned around to pace, that was the moment I acted.

I stepped forward. She turned back at the movement but things were already going too fast to stop. I grabbed on to her wrist, pushing it upward. An unholy scream erupted, my head throbbing from being so close to the source as Sara pulled the trigger. A shockwave coursed through my body as the bullet exploded into my ceiling. The noise, and the fact Sara had really loaded a gun, made me sick as the world shook around me. Dizziness swarmed inside. I couldn't afford to lose focus now. But it got the best of me as I stumbled away, trying to put distance between us, only to go crashing into Sara, and sent us both to the ground.

Fingernails dug into my clothes so close to piercing my skin as Sara gripped on to me before she pushed me off of her. She stood up a lot faster than I could. She wasn't as affected by the explosion as I had been. Sara was far more familiar with guns than I had ever been.

"Look what you did!" she screamed as she pointed the gun down at me, right between my eyes once more. This time, I stared again into the barrel of the gun, watching my life flash before my eyes. There was nothing else I could do.

A jingling bell pierced the peace I had made in my mind, followed by the sound of something smacking against something else. Both Sara and I craned our heads to see two figures bolting through the front door of my shop straight towards us. One had a gun pulled out, and the other was running right into Sara, knocking her right to the ground.

"Warren," I muttered as I watched him put his weight on Sara, forcing her to stay on the floor. The gun had clattered to the ground from the tussle, giving Officer Erickson enough time to run up and kick the gun away.

"Get Ms. Wayward out of here while I wait for backup."

Warren nodded in acknowledgment as he stood, leaving Sara lying on the ground staring up into the barrel of Officer Erickson's gun. Warren walked over to me, his arms wrapping around me as he helped lift me to my feet before helping me walk out of the shop. I wasn't sure I could trust my legs at this moment, not when I had been so close to death. Already a crowd had formed outside as everyone peered inside to see what was going on.

"Are you okay?" Warren whispered as he gently led me to the curb so I could sit down.

"I think so."

I wasn't sure if I was fully okay, but I would have to be. Despite almost meeting death, I couldn't help but think back to the cards. Sara had been right. The Fool. Wheel of Fortune. The World. We'd both stepped close to the cliff, naïve of the upcoming journey we were embarking on. The past had caught up to us, and what goes around must come back around. And finally closure. The ties between our family had been closed. The Wayward curse had been debunked. The cause of Isaac's death had finally been solved.

Chapter 27

I stood in the back of the shop, in the magic room that held the cauldron, fumbling with the boxes that were stacked back here, doing my best trying to locate the items that would be of use now that I was finally able to start making products—no point in buying everything from scratch if some things could be salvaged—when my fingers brushed against something, the silky-smooth fabric of an item that I was familiar with. With a tug, I pulled it out of the box. The piece folded as it slid between the items till it was able to unfurl in the air.

"A hat," I whispered.

Not just any hat, a witch's hat. The memory of my grandmother wearing this very hat while she stood over the cauldron popped into my head. She was fast at work stirring up whatever potion she worked on that day as I sat on a stool nearby watching her. My chest clenched, as years ago I had stepped away from this part of my life and now here I was, ready to embrace the magic that had never left. With sure hands, I set the hat on my head and glanced at myself in the small mirror hanging on the wall. An orange buckle wrapped around the base added just a smidgen of color as I reflected in the instant change in my appearance.

This is Serafina Wayward.

The person I was always meant to be.

A soft jingle filled the air as I rushed out from the back room to the front of the shop to see who had walked in, almost instantly locking eyes with Warren, who had a huge smile already on his face.

"Nice hat."

"Thanks. It was my grandmother's," I answered as I reached up and ran my fingers across the fabric.

He held up a bag. "I brought some sweets." And made his way over to the counter, where he set the bag down. Without waiting for me, he started to pull out two small boxes that had been safely tucked away. "Is the shop open for business yet?"

"It will be soon," I replied as I walked up to the counter to see what sugary goods Warren had brought me. "As soon as I figure out how to make something."

Thank you for reading Mad as a Hatter! If you loved this book, please consider leaving a review! Reviews are important to indie authors as it helps others find my books!

If you are ready for another adventure, dive into Pick Your Poison, the second book in the series! Order here:

Join my newsletter to stay in touch!

Pick Your Poison

Discarding old items could spell ruin for me.

Wayward's Shop of Mysteries is open for business, and I couldn't be more excited. The shelves may be empty now, but they won't be that way for long.

My first spell will change everything, but unfortunately, before I can cast my first spell, things go horribly wrong.

When the residents of Snowton Heights fall ill one right after another, there's one common denominator – a bottle from my shop. Rumors fly that I am behind the mysterious poison. I must clear my name before any more bodies drop.

About Author

Iris Leigh stumbled upon the genre of cozy mystery by accident. Since Iris is easily scared she does her best to avoid horror books, tv shows, and films. But dying for some type of mystery without all the suspense to make her heart burst from terror was when someone asked if she had ever read a cozy mystery. Now she has fallen in love with the genre and started to write to bring her stories to life.

If you want to stay in contact with Iris and learn about upcoming releases, make sure to sign up for the newsletter! You can sign up by navigating to her website!

Website: www.irisleigh.com